AND THE CORPSE WORE TARTAN

By Stuart MacBride

The Logan McRae Books
Cold Granite
Dying Light
Broken Skin
Flesh House
Blind Eye
Dark Blood
Shatter the Bones
Close to the Bone
22 Dead Little Bodies
The Missing and the Dead
In the Cold Dark Ground
The Blood Road
All That's Dead
This House of Burning Bones

Steel & Tufty Books
Now We Are Dead
And the Corpse Wore Tartan

fits here in the timeline

The Ash Henderson Books
Birthdays for the Dead
A Song for the Dying
The Coffinmaker's Garden

The Oldcastle Books
A Dark So Deadly
No Less the Devil
In a Place of Darkness

Standalone
The Dead of Winter

Other Works
Sawbones (a novella)
12 Days of Winter (a short-story collection)
Partners in Crime (two Logan and Steel short stories)
The 45% Hangover (a Logan and Steel novella)
The Completely Wholesome Adventures of Skeleton Bob (a picture book)

Writing as Stuart B. MacBride
Halfhead

AND THE CORPSE WORE TARTAN

Stuart MacBride

MACMILLAN

First published 2026 by Macmillan
an imprint of Pan Macmillan
The Smithson, 6 Briset Street, London EC1M 5NR
EU representative: Macmillan Publishers Ireland Ltd, 1st Floor,
The Liffey Trust Centre, 117–126 Sheriff Street Upper,
Dublin 1 D01 YC43
Associated companies throughout the world

ISBN 978-1-0350-8770-9 HB
ISBN 978-1-0350-8771-6 TPB

Copyright © Stuart MacBride 2026

The right of Stuart MacBride to be identified as the
author of this work has been asserted in accordance
with the Copyright, Designs and Patents Act 1988.

All rights reserved. No part of this publication may be reproduced,
stored in a retrieval system, or transmitted, in any form, or by any means
(including, without limitation, electronic, mechanical, photocopying, recording
or otherwise) without the prior written permission of the publisher.

The quotation 'Theirs not to make reply/Theirs not to reason why/Theirs but to do
and die/Into the valley of Death/Rode the six hundred' is from Alfred Lord Tennyson's
'The Charge of the Light Brigade', first published in
The Examiner, 9 December 1854.

Pan Macmillan does not have any control over, or any responsibility for,
any author or third-party websites (including, without limitation, URLs,
emails and QR codes) referred to in or on this book.

1 3 5 7 9 8 6 4 2

A CIP catalogue record for this book is available from the British Library.

Typeset by Palimpsest Book Production Ltd, Falkirk, Stirlingshire
Printed and bound in the UK using
100% Renewable Electricity by CPI Group (UK) Ltd

This book is sold subject to the condition that it shall not, by way of
trade or otherwise, be lent, hired out, or otherwise circulated without
the publisher's prior consent in any form of binding or cover other than
that in which it is published and without a similar condition including
this condition being imposed on the subsequent purchaser. The publisher does
not authorize the use or reproduction of any part of this book in any manner
for the purpose of training artificial intelligence technologies or systems.
The publisher expressly reserves this book from the Text and Data Mining
exception in accordance with Article 4(3) of the European Union
Digital Single Market Directive 2019/790.

Visit **www.panmacmillan.com** to read more about all our books
and to buy them.

For Sarah
(who went to work with the crows...)

— foreshadowing —

The book you now hold in your hands is my homage to the Golden Age of detective fiction.

I've loved crime fiction ever since I was a little boy. When I was handed my school library card, the first thing I did was blitz my way through all the Hardy Boys novels, by Franklin W. Dixon (who turned out to be a committee of writers for hire – a bit like a large number of squirrels, squeezed into a trench coat and snap-brim fedora, passing themselves off as a hard-bitten PI on the mean streets of Plockton).

Night after night, when everyone else was abed, and I was meant to be asleep, I'd be huddled under the duvet, reading about solving crimes and having adventures. Then, after devouring everything the committee/squirrels had written, I moved on to Dashiell Hammett's *Red Harvest*. Bit of a jump, but I bloody *loved* that book. It led me to *The Maltese Falcon*, *The Dain Curse*, and *The Glass Key*. And I was off, roaming the library shelves: Raymond Chandler, Daphne du Maurier, Reginald Hill, Ruth Rendell, Arthur Conan Doyle, Patricia Highsmith… All of them different, all of them bringing something exciting and new.

And we can't forget the Queen of Crime™ herself: Dame Agatha Mary Clarissa Christie DBE. With her strange little detectives that have cast a long, murderous shadow over much of British crime fiction ever since…

Which brings us to *And the Corpse Wore Tartan* – after all, the story's set in a fancy castle hotel, in a remote part of Scotland, where the landed gentry have gathered to celebrate a wedding. Throw in a man with a funny moustache, or a nosy old lady who has a penchant for tweed, and you have the perfect set-up for primetime-Sunday-evening-wholesome-for-all-the-family entertainment.

Only I had to go and ruin it by adding Detective Sergeant Roberta Steel to the mix.

When I first introduced her in *Cold Granite*, all those years ago, she was a chain-smoking, wrinkly (because of all the chain smoking), foul-mouthed, rule-breaking, lascivious horror. And so much *fun* to write!

She was created to be the antithesis of DI Insch. He was a proper by-the-book copper, stern and quick to anger, but fair, while Steel was anything but. They were the demon and angel on Logan's shoulders, or, if you want to get all Freudian about it: Insch was Logan's superego, urging him to stay on the path of righteousness; Steel was Logan's id, urging him to cut corners, go to the pub, and eat loads of deep-fried things. Pulling him in opposite and frequently impossible directions. Psychomachia, writ large!

As the books went on, she mellowed a bit. Stopped womanising and settled down. Got married. Her wife, Susan, has given birth to two kids, so Steel's had to stop smoking and swearing, but she's kept her rather ... *unique* view of the world and acerbic wit.

Way back in 2007, the lovely Andrew Taylor, in *The Spectator*, said of Roberta's third outing: 'DI Steel should be declared a national treasure.' I'm not entirely sure what she'd make of being placed in the same category as Thora Hird and Tommy Cooper, but *I* like it.

And now she has a book of her very own (after having to share *Now We Are Dead* with Tufty).

I wrote *And the Corpse Wore Tartan* just before the first COVID lockdown, which is why some things aren't mentioned here that you might otherwise expect. I suppose, in its way, it's now a historical crime novel, set in the days before the world decided to really embrace stupidity, populism, and being a *massive* dick. At the time, I was aiming for a nice wee novella that Sarah Hodgson and I could work on, before she departed for pastures new.

You see, Sarah was my editor at HarperCollins for over a decade (I know, I know, she deserves a medal for putting up with me for so long). She left HC after an astonishing twenty-one years to conquer new and different publishing worlds. And I wanted to mark our time together with one last fun little project before she went.

Clearly, *And the Corpse Wore Tartan* grew slightly longer legs than I'd anticipated. Then longer still. Then it got itself some stilts and went striding about the Scottish countryside, hurling obscenities at the squirrels, eventually coming home at a beefy fifty-three-and-a-bit thousand words – which is technically a novel. Albeit a short one. Which I now present for your edification and amusement.

So, make yourself a nice cup of tea, get yourself a biscuit (a tasty one, maybe with jam and/or chocolate), and settle down for a tale of criminal naughtiness, in the company of Detective Sergeant Roberta Steel…

— the mourning after the night before —

1

The woman's body lies on its back in the long grass, a pale slash of belly on show between the rumpled shirt and stained trousers. A flash of bra – the colour of old bones. Milkbottle skin speckled with tiny dots of red. One leg curled under the other. One arm stretched out in accusation. Head thrown back, mouth open. As if she's been *screaming*.

Albert Nairn moves the shotgun to his other hand, the barrel still warm to the touch, that bitter-sweet scent of a recently fired cartridge. The smell of death.

Up above, the sky is a lid of dark greys and funeral blues, thick with heavy clouds. A faint bloody glow oozing its way along the horizon, not bright enough to taint the sickly grey light.

Not bright enough to illuminate the body.

Hmph...

He prods it with the shotgun.

Nothing.

Checks his watch, 04:28.

Better get her moved before the guests wake up. That'll ruin someone's morning – throwing open the curtains to find a dead woman on the lawn.

There's a flicker of white, followed by a rumble of thunder, and a thin, cold rain. Pattering down around the body, making the grass quiver and bend, as if it's in mourning.

No point standing here, Albert. Get her up and over your shoulder. Take her back to the cottage, where no one will ever find her – there's plenty of room in his collection for one more corpse. Big day today, why spoil it by getting the police involved?

The rain thickens, getting into its stride, falling on the living and the dead alike.

Come on then.

He bends down, reaching...

And that's when the body gasps and sits up, eyes wide and bloodshot, grey hair sticking out like she's been dragged through every hedge in the place.

Roberta blinked as an auld mannie, in tweeds and wellies, screamed like a wee girl and danced away from her. The shotgun he was holding clunked down on the wet grass, freeing up both hands to clutch at his grey beard and tartan bunnet.

Then the ache hit her. The throbbing *pounding* horror headache from hell, swelling up inside her skull and threatening to push both her eyeballs out through her nose. Tongue like a mouldy flip-flop marinated in someone else's vomit, then set on fire. Stomach like a washing machine full of bricks and bees as the world went into spin cycle around her.

Don't be sick, don't be sick, don't be sick.

Instead a lung-rattling bout of coughing got its oar in, ending with something the size and colour of an oyster being spat out into the undergrowth.

Urgh...

'Holy mother of God...' The old man bent double, holding onto his knees, peering at her with yellowy eyes set either side of a great curved hook of a nose. 'Scared the hairy *arse* off us!'

Roberta screwed one eye shut and tried to get the world to stop whirling. Grabbing a handful of grass so she wouldn't fall off and tumble away into the battleship sky. 'Am I...' She cleared her throat and tried again. 'Am I dead?'

'Come on, let's get you up.'

A rough, calloused paw grabbed her arm and hauled her to her feet. Which, to be honest, just made the whirling worse.

Didn't help that her legs were malfunctioning. Rotten pair of bastards refused to work properly, making her lurch into a wobbly stagger. Which—

Rancid gurgling erupted from her stomach, heat flushing through her neck and head.

Don't be sick!

The auld mannie let go and scampered back a bit. 'No, no, no, no, no...'

She swallowed it down, held up a hand, and huffed out a few deep breaths.

If she wasn't dead, she was dying. This hangover was terminal, no doubt about it.

Which, if anything, was a relief if it meant the suffering would end.

A rumbling *BOOOM* made the air shake, jabbing red-hot knives through her forehead and out the other side.

Death was taking his own sweet time coming.

The auld mannie bent down and picked an empty bottle from the undergrowth, turning it in his hands. 'Lagavulin, sixteen-year-old. You drink all of this?' He whistled low and slow. 'No wonder you smell like a skip full of burnt mattresses.'

A whole bottle of Lagavulin? Oh God.

Why would... Where was...

She did a one-legged lurcharound, keeping the other one firmly locked and straight.

Ah.

An ugly stately-home castle thing loomed in the rain, its thick stone walls painted a cheery shade of pinky beige. Turrets. Mullioned windows. It lay at the far end of a manicured lawn, framed by thick pine forests with a background of purple-flecked mountains – their tops lost in the low cloud. Sort of a Marks & Spencer shortbread tin designed by Hammer House of Horror.

They'd lumped a conservatory on the side, with 'Skirivour Castle Hotel' printed in big gold letters on a dark green sign.

Oh no.

Lightning strobed the hillside, bringing with it a hissing clatter, followed by a headache-punishing *BOOOOOOO-OOOOOM*. Then the rain *really* got to work, battering down on the world in general and Roberta in particular. Because Mother Nature was a vindictive cow who hated her.

The auld mannie pointed at a door marked 'FIRE EXIT'. 'Best get inside and dry, lass, afore you catch your death.'

If only he knew, there was a fate *worse* than death in there waiting for her...

Gah... How much tartan did one hotel need? Whole place was clarted in the damned stuff. Tartan carpet, tartan wallpaper, tartan furnishings. You'd have to be a sadist to design something like this. What about poor people with hangovers? Did no one ever think about them?

Roberta lurched down the corridor, one hand scuffing along the wall for balance.

And the stuffed animals were creepy too.

Look at them, staring out at her with their beady glass eyes from their bell jars and display cases. Wild cats, foxes, every variety of Scottish bird you could shoot. Stags' heads on the wall, mouths hanging open in surprised disappointment.

The corridor ended in a narrow set of stairs, which were far too steep for normal human beings WITH SODDING HANGOVERS.

She stopped to catch her breath halfway up.

More lumbering growls from her itchy stomach.

Serve them right if she blew chunks all over their tartan horror house.

But then that would land her in even more trouble, wouldn't it? And she was in enough shite as it was.

Roberta reached the top of the stairs without redecorating them, then staggered along the corridor. They'd cut back on the tartan here. A bit. The carpet was still migraine-inducing, but at least the walls were a womblike dark burgundy. Even if the flock wallpaper was verruca ugly. It set off the nasty oil paintings of twee Scottish scenes. Oh, come away in, you'll have had your *tea*, Hamish. Och, I'd love to, Agnes, but I've got this stag to hump.

She dug her key out of her jacket pocket – complete with stupid great-big wooden key fob.

What kind of idiot didn't put numbers on their hotel rooms?

Look at this lot: 'BALVENIE', 'BENROMACH', 'ARDBEG', 'GLENDRONACH'... How the hell were you supposed to find your room? They weren't even themed! Where are you staying? Oh, I'm in the Speyside malts. See, that would make *sense*. These were all over the shop.

Another sign at the end of the corridor had 'RECEPTION ↘' on it, but next to that was the one that matched her stupid key fob: 'LAPHROAIG'.

Roberta unlocked the door and stumbled inside. Thumped it shut behind her. Leaned back against it and let out a shuddery foul-tasting breath.

The curtains were drawn, making the room a gloomy obstacle course, but there was no mistaking the massive bed with its flouncy canopy. She hauled off her soggy jacket and shirt, dumping them both on the floor, kicked off her wet shoes, and staggered over. Timbered facedown onto the bed with a mournful groan.

'I'm dying...'

Susan sat up. Could feel her doing it. *And* the completely unsympathetic daggers she was *definitely* glaring into Roberta's back. Heartless monster that she was.

And then, to prove it, she shoved Roberta off the bed, sending her crashing down on the horrible tartan carpet.

'Nooo...'

'Shhh!'

And when Roberta wobbled to her knees and peered over the edge, Susan was already lying flat and rigid, like a coffin lid, seething. A sadistic *tut*, then she turned her back and hauled the duvet over her again.

It was enough to make you...

Oh no.

Roberta crawled away as fast as possible, through the door to the en suite and its big Victorian toilet, yanked the lid up and spattered every single internal organ she owned into it.

Rain rattled the bathroom window as Roberta surfaced from the toilet bowl. Coming up for air that stank of rancid bitter yuck. Flushing helped. But not much.

They'd abandoned the tartan theme in here, going instead for that palette of muted greys hotels like so much. Lots of really expensive tiles. A big enamel bath. And a mini wet-room-shower-thing in the corner. White fluffy bathrobes hanging on the back of the door, embroidered with the Laird's coat of arms to make sure everyone knew how swanky Skirivour Castle Hotel was.

The robes swished from side to side as Susan barged the door open for a good glower. It put wrinkles on her slightly rounded face, stealing away some of the prettiness. Her blonde, middle-aged Doris-Day-in-Calamity-Jane kind of look was a bit undermined by the red babydoll nightie, but she still had cracking legs.

Susan folded her arms, making her bosom heave up.

And talking of heaving...

Roberta stuck her head back down the toilet and gave it another filling. Ended with a wee sob that echoed back from her porcelain prison. 'Can you at least hold my hair back?'

'Hold your own bloody hair.'

Nooo...

'How *could* you embarrass me like that, Robbie? How? I have to *work* with these people!'

Every retch was like being kicked in the stomach by an angry horse.

'You never think of *anyone* but yourself, do you? I just don't count. If it's not about *you* it might as well never bloody happen. You behaved appallingly!'

Roberta surfaced from the toilet's depths, resting her cheek against the wooden seat. Warm and comforting from all the bums that had sat on it. 'I... I am always on my best... best behaviour...'

'You don't remember, do you? You're *impossible*!'

Remember? What was there to remember?

Lurching up to the bar and banging her empty glass down, setting little bowls of macadamia nuts dancing. Struggling to make the words sound right. ''Nother whisky!'

Flailing her limbs about as 'Come on Eileen' belts out of the DJ's speakers; all the Tweedy Twats and Strapless Sharons in their wedding outfits staring at her like she's some sort of leper, just cos she's having a good time and singing along.

Hauling back a hand and slapping that smug git Sir Reginald Bradbury-Scott right in his smug fat face, hard enough to make him land on his smug fat arse.

Stumbling out of the conservatory, stiff-legged like a drunken chicken, clutching a bottle of pilfered Lagavulin, swigging from it as she marches off into the darkness...

Oh.

Roberta wiped the slime from her mouth and spat into the toilet bowl. Did her best nonchalant shrug. 'I might have had a *little* bit to drink, but I didn't do anything that—'

'Impossible!' Susan stormed out of the bathroom, slamming the door behind her, setting the fluffy bathrobes swinging again.

Clearly, she hadn't understood just how ill Roberta was.

Deep breath. 'I NEED IRN-BRU! AND MAYBE SOME BACON? I could go bacon…' Another horrible gurgling noise erupted deep inside. 'Hold on.' She gripped the wooden seat and swallowed hard. No more being sick. No more being sick. No more being sick. 'Urgh…'

Susan reappeared in the doorway, eyes blazing, mouth all pinched up like an angry fish. Voice a hard, hissing whisper: 'It's five in the morning; will you keep your bloody voice down!' She turned to leave, then turned back. 'And if you think I'm taking you to another wedding, or anywhere else, *ever* again, you can roll it sideways and cram it up there!'

Wait, what?

'Wedding?' As soon as the word left Roberta's bitter-yuck-flavoured mouth, it all came flooding back. She screwed her whole face shut. 'Oh God…'

The horror.

THE HORROR!

2

A happy sun blazed away in the bright blue sky, happy fluffy wee clouds making happy fluffy shapes as Roberta's MX-5 roared along the winding road. Got to give it to those tartan Highland buggers, they know how to do scenery. Heather-clad hills in full purple bloom, a shimmering loch, swathes of deep-green forests... Some sort of eagly thing wheeling overhead. Idiot sheep taking a break from doing whatever it was idiot sheep did to watch her wee sports car flash past.

Top down, music on, singing along with Lemmy on 'Ace of Spades'.

Couldn't get much better than that, could you?

She stuck her foot down.

Hills crowded in on either side, then the road twisted around to the left and the whole thing opened up. A valley, guarded by regimented ranks of Forestry Commission pines, all standing to attention in the sunshine. And smack bang in the middle of it: Skirivour Castle, just visible over the treetops.

OK, so it wasn't the prettiest castle – more Frankenstein than Disney – but they'd painted it a pinky-gold colour that looked jaunty among all that verdant greenery.

The road wound down the valley side, to a high-arched

bridge spanning a deep gully and a swollen river. All very picturesque as Roberta wheeched over it and into the woods. Following the signs, music belting out.

A set of huge stone pillars rose on either side of the narrow road, with 'Skirivour Castle Hotel' picked out in wrought-iron letters across the top.

To be honest, the castle wasn't any prettier up close. It sulked at the end of its wide gravel driveway, a drooping fountain splashing out the kind of feeble stream that implied it needed a visit to the doctor's, where someone barely out of medical school would snap on a rubber glove and stick a finger up its bum.

Union flags fluttered from poles, flanking a pillared portico that was big enough for an eightsome reel. Someone had draped the thing in a whole heap of red-white-and-blue bunting, and clusters of gold balloons bobbed in the air – above weights wrapped like wedding presents. Bet there were doves somewhere. Places like this *loved* doves.

A sign pointed to a gap in the hedge: 'Resident And Guest Parking'. Course, the temptation was just to abandon her MX-5 in front of the main doors, but that wasn't really in the spirit of the thing, was it? So she parked in the far corner of the designated spaces, like a good little girl, next to a *very* expensive-looking Jag and a couple of Porsches.

Stuck the roof up.

Popped the boot and grabbed her luggage.

Sauntered back to the castle's entrance.

Pushed through the ornate carved double doors, and into a *massive* lobby.

It was at least three-storeys tall, the floor covered in a red-and-yellow tartan carpet that probably seemed like a good idea at the time. But the thing that really stood out was the huge metal stag that dominated the space. Thing had to be twice the size of a real stag, if not more, looming over everything from its six-foot-tall plinth in full *Monarch of the Glen* pose.

It wasn't alone in here either. Every wall and flat surface in the place was crowded with stuffed boars' heads and stags' heads and pheasants and grouse and hares and all the rest. As if someone had gone out and slaughtered every animal on the estate then carted it off wholesale to the nearest taxidermist.

Whole heap of oil paintings too – the kind that got printed onto coasters and sold in museum gift shops. Couple of tapestries. A bunch of claymores and shields and halberds. Twin suits of armour stood guard at the bottom of a sweeping wooden staircase that curled away to the balconies running along both sides of the lobby.

Like... Like Hollywood's idea of how Scotland was meant to look. Brigadoon, with even more kitsch.

A wee man appeared at her elbow, done up in full Highland regalia, complete with pointy bunnet that had feathers poking out of it. Not the best outfit for someone who looked as if they were made of wrinkles, bones, and string. His voice trembled more than his hands as he pointed at a silver tray with a bottle and some cut-crystal tumblers on it. 'Would you care for a complimentary welcome dram? It's a twelve-year-old Glenfeòrag, made just down the road.'

Now, *that* was more like it.

Roberta rubbed her hands together. 'Ho, ho, don't mind if I—'

A voice cut across The Lobby That Brigadoon Forgot. *'Roberta?'* Sounding a bit shocked.

She pivoted around and there was Susan, marching towards her, in jeans and a floral shirt, hair up in a 'do' that was far too fancy for what she was wearing. Voice a sharp-edged whisper. 'What are you doing here?'

Roberta preened a little. 'Decided to surprise you. Wee romantic gesture, and all that.' Threw in a little swagger and a dig in the ribs for good measure. 'You're welcome.'

'You said you weren't coming! You're not on the guest...' Her eyes bugged as one of those strapping athletic types wandered into the room.

Now, being a professional police officer, you notice certain wee details that would probably pass your ordinary punter by, but to a *trained* eye, one with decades of experience in law enforcement – going by the big white meringue-style dress she was wearing – Little Miss Athletic was probably getting married today. It was an off-the-shoulder job, exposing a delicious amount of cleavage that swelled and wobbled as she breathed. Attractive, in a broad-shouldered-could-snap-you-in-two kind of way, even with her hair still in rollers.

Probably liked being spanked. The bossy ones always did.

Susan grabbed Roberta's hand. 'Don't you *dare* embarrass me!' Then raised her voice to a more normal and cheery volume, waving at the bride-to-be. 'Adriana!'

Athletic Adriana turned and beamed at her, sweeping in for a hug. 'Susan!' She pulled a constipated-frog face, arms out. 'What do you think of the dress, is it too froofie-meringue-bums? I think it's a bit froofie, but it's my wedding day and if you can't be froofie on your wedding day, when can you?'

The two of them shared a mwah-mwah air kiss.

Then Athletic Adriana finally noticed Roberta. Stared for a moment, then went back to Susan. 'Oh. But I thought you...?'

'Adriana, you remember my wife, Roberta Steel?' Pulling on a smile that looked a bit pained. 'She decided it would be *romantic* to surprise me and come after all. After *telling* me she *had* to be at a training conference all weekend.' Was that a note of disapproval in her voice? 'And couldn't make it.'

Nah, course it wasn't. That was the problem with big romantic gestures, some people took a while to get over the shock.

Roberta treated Athletic Adriana to a swaggery head wobble too. 'Wee white lie. You know, for romantic purposes.'

And for some reason, Susan mouthed 'Sorry!' at the bride-to-be.

Weird.

There was a pause, then Adriana had a bash at a none-too-convincing smile of her own. 'I see. How ... lovely.'

'Nothing's too good for my main squeeze.' And to prove the point, Roberta grabbed a handful of Susan's bum and gave it a squeezing.

Which made her go bright pink and mouth, 'Sorry!' again.

A couple of blinks and Adriana seemed to get it together. 'Oh, yah, you're the police officer, right? We met ... at the work's Christmas bash? Yes. Glad you could join us after all.' Then went in for one of those ridiculous mwah-mwah kisses.

Yeah, not playing that game.

But it did give Roberta a really good look down the front of her dress.

Magnificent boobage.

The mwah-mwahs over, she turned back to Susan. 'Nobody told me getting married was a *total* organisational nightmarefest! The wedding planner's broken her leg, Mummy's gone *complete* meltdown because of the centrepieces, Daddy's disappeared, and I'm supposed to be having a nice relaxing bath, instead of stomping about like an *absolute* Bridezilla in my dress! But there's a *million* things to do,' sideways glance in Roberta's direction, 'like *reorganise* the seating plan. And I haven't even had my hair styled yet. Disasterama!'

Susan took both of her hands. 'I'm here to help. What needs doing?'

'Oh, you're just the best boss *ever*!' She actually welled up a bit at that.

'Robbie, why don't you go check in and freshen up?' Susan stuck her chin in the air. 'I've got some bottom to kick.'

And with that, the pair of them swept off, laughing, leaving Roberta alone with Captain String-and-Bones.

He cleared his throat and held out one of those crystal tumblers, a teeny finger of molten amber sloshing about at the bottom of the trembling glass. 'Madam?'

'Better make it a double...'

Well, that wasn't a sight to inspire confidence, was it?

A fat, wrinkly, half-naked horror stared back at her from the hotel-room mirror. It wasn't even a proper bra, just a set of twin black lace-and-netting hammocks with teeny wee straps. Not an underwire to its name. And the *pants*! Brazilians were meant to be when you got a butch woman called Helga to rip the hairs off your undercarriage, so you didn't look like you were smuggling a sasquatch down the front of your bikini – Brazilians weren't meant to be pants. Oh, yeah, they *looked* like decent-sized pants, but that didn't stop the middle bit from disappearing right up your bumcrack.

Roberta hauled it out again.

And the *state* of her...

Black lace against fish-belly skin. *So* much fish-belly skin.

She gave her fancy new underwear a shoogle, setting up a sympathetic sine wave in her not-so-taut areas. Wobble, wobble, wobble, wobble, wobble.

No doubt about it: she looked ridiculous in this get-up. Mutton dressed as spam.

Urgh...

Roberta took a double handful of pasty stomach, pulled it up, and let it thump-wobble down again. Grimacing as the ripples subsided.

She let loose a big, heavy sigh, making the lacy hammocks sag.

'Fat. Wrinkly. Old. And horrible...'

The pants were bad enough, but the bra? What the hell had Susan been thinking? You'd have to be a flat-chested stick insect to fit into the damned thing. Roberta wriggled out of it and hurled the lacy disaster into her open suitcase, where it could bloody well stay. She'd be wearing Old Faithful for the duration, thank you very much.

She checked her watch: half one.

Urgh...

Better get dressed quick, before Susan appeared and discovered there wasn't going to be any black-lacy-boob-hammock-horror going on.

Don't want to spoil the mystery, after all.

The queue of guests snaked ahead of Roberta and Susan, heading for the on-site chapel, all the way through the hotel lobby and out the front door. The men a mixture of starchy Highland dress and clashing kilts, the women in weird cocktail-dress/ball-gown hybrids topped off with ridiculous hats.

Susan had opted for the nice purple dress that made her bum and boobs look eminently nibbleable. Roberta squeezed herself into the bright-blue suit that Susan always *said* she liked, but kinda felt a bit like wearing the TARDIS. While those rotten Brazilian pants embarked on their fifteenth attempt at a lacy colonoscopy in the last four minutes. Should have swapped the bloody things for a nice comfy pair of massive pants when she'd ditched their horrible-hammock friend, but it was too late now.

'Could I no' have worn jeans and T-shirt?'

'You look *lovely*.'

The queue shuffled forwards.

Roberta dug the Brazilian out of her crack again. 'Feel like a right prick in this.'

'Will you leave your undercarriage alone?'

'All right for you, your pants aren't trying to disappear up your bumhole.'

They passed a perky wee thing in a *very* low-cut dress. Lovely tanned cleavage, hair swept up in a wobbly tower of blonde. Not bad looking either, if you liked them early-twenties and clarted in YouTube-make-up-tutorial slap. Pacing up and down the tartan carpet, checking her watch, hurling angry glances at front door.

Roberta leaned in close to Susan's ear, eyebrows jigging up and down. 'Corrrrr ... I would, wouldn't you?'

Face dead ahead, not even looking at Little Miss Perky. 'Behave yourself!'

'Bet she wriggles like an eel on a washing machine if you do her right.'

'Robbie!'

A grin. 'Could eat cottage cheese off that pert wee arse all night long.' Not the stuff with pineapple in it, though, that would just be perverse. 'Think she's a screamer? I think she's a screamer.'

Susan's voice dropped to an angry whisper. 'I have to *work* with these people!'

Another young woman rocked up to them: ginger hair, freckles, and a tartan miniskirt – proffering glasses of sparkly drinks on a big silver tray. She was probably going for a welcoming smile, but it came off a bit serial-killery. 'Champagne or Buck's Fizz?'

Roberta helped herself to two glasses of pale-golden fizz. 'Ta.' Then nodded at Susan. 'You want one too?'

'You are *not* to get drunk and humiliate me, Robbie. I swear, if you do…'

'Ah well, all the more for me.' She scoofed half of the first glass, stifling the resulting belch because this was clearly meant to be a classy do.

Up ahead, the queue parted as a lanky PC, wearing the full Police Scotland uniform, stumbled in through the doors, against the flow of people. 'Pardon me, scuse me…' He'd accessorised the black T-shirt, peaked cap, and itchy trousers with this season's must-haves – a utility belt, stabproof vest, and high-vis waistcoat. A suit carrier draped over one shoulder, a rucksack held in the other hand. Thin, and Adam's appley, with a close-cropped head of ginger hair. Like Irn-Bru-coloured suede.

'Barbara!' He lankied over to Miss Perky-Cleavage, all hangdog and puppy-eyed. 'I'm sorry, I'm sorry…'

'Where the hell have you been?' She jabbed a finger at the queue. 'It's starting!'

'It's all the rain. Bob Ronnach's farm's flooded, we had to rescue his sheep. They're talking about the reservoir bursting and—'

Her finger came around and poked him instead. 'If you make me late for my *brother's wedding*, Michael McKinnon, I'm going to skin you alive and make you eat the bits!'

'Sorry, sorry, I'll be a flash, I swear!' And with that, he scurried off up the big wooden staircase, taking it two steps at a time.

Miss Perky-Cleavage scowled after him. 'Men!'

Aha.

Roberta gave her a wave, throwing in a wee leer for good luck. 'Serve him right if you join the Sapphic Sisterhood,

Babs. We've got very good introductory offers and an excellent mentoring programme.'

Susan's elbow jabbed into Roberta's ribs. 'I said, don't embarrass me!'

'Ask us about our First-Time-Lesbian Starter-Pack specials!'

Barbara, AKA: Miss Perky, stuck her nose in the air and flounced off after her lanky PC.

Ah well, couldn't convert them all. Not on the *first* go.

Roberta grinned. 'I like 'em feisty.'

Susan just glared at her.

3

Gah... It was boiling in here.

Sunlight streamed through the high, stained-glass windows, painting the pews and their occupants in vibrant rainbow colours. Like a really stuffy Pride parade, populated with middle-aged tosspots. Had to be at least two hundred of them, crammed into the chapel, listening to the fat old git up front droning on and on about the benefits and blessings of marriage.

No way he was a day under seventy-five. Bet he hadn't seen his willy for at least two decades, and if he did there wouldn't be enough Viagra in the world to make it sit up and beg.

Roberta wriggled in her seat, trying to work those damned pants out of her crack by the power of friction alone, because apparently it was bad manners to dig at your bumhole in church. As if an all-seeing God didn't already know you had half a pair of Brazilian pants wedged where the sun seldom shone.

The bride was growing on her though, standing up there with that magnificent boobage all blue and gold in the stained light. Beaming. 'I do!'

The lucky sod she was marrying had the floppy-brown hair of a public schoolboy, broad shoulders, upright bearing – as if someone had jammed a flagpole up his rear-end – and, shockingly enough, actually looked good in the full kilt get-up.

Even if he *was* wearing one of those oh-so-slapable, ain't-I-the-greatest? smiles.

'Excellent, excellent.' The minister raised his liver-spotted hands to the congregation. 'And will you, Adriana and Douglas's family and friends, love and support them in their union?'

The whole lot of them belted it out as one: 'We will.'

Saps.

Roberta puffed out her cheeks and rolled her eyes. Kept her voice quiet as a mouse's fart, 'Whatever happened to the "speak now or forever hold your piece" bit?'

But Susan wasn't taking her on – sitting there sniffling into a hankie, as if this pair of twazzocks were Romeo and Juliet.

'"Aye, I'm here to sweep the bride off her feet and into a bathtub full of Nutella and seedless raspberry jam!"'

'Then,' Fat-Boy gave them all a flash of his dentures, 'by the power vested in me by the Lord our God, I hereby pronounce you husband and wife!'

A cheer went up from the congregation.

Roberta leaned in for another go. 'Course, it makes your bits all sticky, but that's a price I'm willing to pay.'

'Will you shut up!'

'You may now kiss the bride.'

Another cheer, as Adriana and Douglas tried to extract each other's wisdom teeth using nothing but their tongues.

Randy sods.

God, other people's weddings were *boring*. Different when it was your own wedding, when you knew everyone and they were all there to shower you with presents and nonstop adulation, but other people's? Strangers droning on and on about wasn't it a lovely day, and I can't believe the weather held off for them, and weren't the bridesmaids to *die* for?

Numpties.

Let's face it: making poor *innocent* people sit through other buggers' weddings was probably against the Geneva Conventions. Bet you could end up in the Hague for that. Especially if you made them wear arse-crack-cheese-wire pants too.

The queue shuffled forward another couple of lengths. Up at the front, a pair of ancient morons in matching tweed peered at the seating board, trying to recognise their own names. How long did it take to work out what table you were sitting on? All going to be dead of old age by the time they got there.

Finally the Tweedies sodded off, and it was Roberta and Susan's turn.

The hotel had mounted a large corkboard on an easel, and decorated it around the outside with blue rosettes – each one with a year printed on it in gold: '2017', '2015', '2010', '1992', '1987', '1983'… No pattern to it at all, but that was weddings for you, wasn't it?

Nineteen big round tables on the accompanying diagram, a rectangular one along the top, and a bunch of names down either side. But whoever printed it out needed a new toner cartridge or something, because the letters were all teeny and indecipherable.

Roberta gave the seating plan a good squint, but it didn't help. 'Where are we sitting?'

'Oh, put your glasses on, for goodness' sake.'

'I don't *need* glasses. It's no' my fault they always print these things in the tiniest font imaginable.'

A sigh, then Susan had a frown at the board. 'You know your problem? You…' Her eyes went wide, her mouth clicked shut, then she turned an ingratiating smile on the next couple in line. 'Please excuse us, we'll just be a minute.' She grabbed Roberta's arm and hustled her away into the corner.

'What? I never did anything!'

A hard, icy whisper: 'Now, you listen to me, Roberta Alexander Steel, you will *behave* yourself in there tonight, do you understand me?'

'Aye, aye.'

'No, not "aye, aye," you swear to me on … on Stalin and Mr Rumpole's lives that you will not *say* or *do* anything that will embarrass me.'

Roberta pulled her chin in. 'Jesus, is there—'

Getting even closer and steelier. 'No matter what happens, you are on your *utmost* best behaviour.' A poke. 'Utmost!'

OK, this was weird, even for Susan. Intense. And … weird.

But hey-ho. Roberta was nothing if not sensitive and flexible.

She nodded. 'All right, I swear. I'll no' do nothing embarrassing.' Pausing for a second to dig those horrible Brazilian pants out of her undercarriage.

'Good. Thank you.' Susan smoothed down Roberta's lapels. 'Come on then.' Took her arm and swept them both into the ballroom.

Very swanky. Well, if your idea of swanky was a large oak-panelled room lined with enough stuffed animals to start a very creepy zoo. There was even a bear in the corner, standing at full stretch, paws and claws out for the lads. More twee oil paintings, medieval weapons, and a big carved coat of arms. All the tables arranged around the outside of a wooden dance floor.

And, if that wasn't swanky enough, a string quartet perched on a podium off to one side, played what sounded like ABBA covers as the assembled idiots meandered to their allotted seats.

Every table but one was decked out in blue. Blue table runners, blue streamers, blue balloons bobbing bluely above blue-themed floral centrepieces. Each with its table name on a sign mounted in the middle, surrounded by bottles of wine and party poppers.

The odd one out was decked in red, for some reason, banished to the opposite corner, by the door marked 'Toilets'.

Susan led the way across to one of the blue tables near the front, where a couple of oldies were already sitting and shaking hands with one another.

Roberta squinted up at the sign – nice big letters, which was a help. Gold on a blue background, like the rosettes. Now, what did it say...? Ah, yes: 'Michael Heseltine'.

Really?

Wait: why would anyone call a table 'Michael Heseltine'?

Didn't make any sense.

She fumbled her glasses from her jacket pocket and stuck them on. Turned to look around the room. Mouth falling open in disbelief. 'Oh, you have *got* to be kidding!'

The next table over was, 'Nigel Lawson'. 'John Major' squatted next to that, then 'Norman Lamont', on and on the horror went: 'Geoffrey Howe', 'Kenneth Clarke', 'Norman Tebbit', 'Douglas Hurd'...

The only table *not* named after a member of Margaret Bloody Thatcher's cabinet was the one draped in red: 'Terrible Trotskyites'.

Roberta pulled off her glasses and stared at Susan. 'You... It's... We...' Mouth working like a drowning goldfish.

'Now, Robbie, you *promised*!'

'It's... We're...'

An older gent in a morning suit appeared from the other side of the table, bringing a matronly woman with him, the pair of them wearing far too much jewellery for people in their mid-sixties. He grabbed Susan for a kiss on the cheek. 'Susan, darling, don't you scrub up well? I mean, it's not like you're a *bag lady* in the office, but—'

'Honestly!' The woman elbowed him. 'Feet out of your mouth, Morty, while you've still got socks on.'

Roberta gawped up at 'MICHAEL HESELTINE' again. 'How could... It's...'

'Ha. Quite right, Agatha. Foot removal it is! Sorry, Susan. Senior partner having a senior moment, there.'

Susan beamed at the pair of them. 'Mortimer, Agatha, wasn't it a lovely ceremony?'

Michael *Heseltine*? 'I can't...'

The Agatha woman gave Susan a mwah-mwah. 'Oh, I was bawling my eyes out the whole way through. Love a good wedding, me.' She turned a Steradent smile on Roberta. 'Agatha Beresford. You must be the famous police hero we've heard so much about!' She moved in for another mwah-mwah.

But Roberta finally got her gob working again: 'It's a Tory wedding! It's all Tories! Everywhere!' Spinning around, staring out at the bastards. 'All of them!'

'Ha, ha...' Susan simpered at Agatha and Mortimer. 'Robbie's such a card, isn't she? If you could excuse us for *just* a second...' She grabbed Roberta's arm again and dragged her off to the middle of the dance floor. 'You *promised*!'

What had that got to do with anything?

'You took me to a Tory wedding! It's wall-to-wall Tories in here! Tories!'

'You promised on Mr Rumpole's life! *And* Stalin's!'

Roberta turned, pointing at the solitary table flying the red flag. 'Why can't we sit with the Terrible Trotskyists?'

That scrawny wee PC was standing beside it. He'd changed out of his police clobber and into a cheap-and-shiny-looking Prince Charlie kilt outfit that he must've hired from someone who hated him. And thought he was three sizes larger. PC Scrawny McCrapKilt pulled out a chair so his boot-faced girlfriend could sit with their fellow non-Tories.

Susan – traitor, quisling, betrayer – adopted a soothing voice. 'It's only for a couple of hours.'

'But I don't *want* to sit on Michael Heseltine!'

And the soothing tone vanished, replaced by one made of frozen reinforced concrete: 'You will sit on Michael Heseltine and like it!'

Michael Heseltine looked as if he'd been on a dirty protest – with multiple gravy, wine, and other assorted stains smeared across him. All the plates cleared away, in favour of tea, coffee, and teeny plates of petits fours.

And the speeches droned on and on and on…

Roberta topped up her glass with yet another hefty slug of shiraz as the father-of-the-bride kept going – standing behind the top table in his morning-suit finery. A chunky monkey with greying sideburns and suspiciously dark hair. Like he'd dipped most of his head in a bucket of Just for Men. Or shoe polish.

Sir Reginald Bradbury-Scott: which had to be one of the most Tory names to ever Tory a Tory. He had one of those accents where every last trace of Scottishness had been sandblasted off by whatever poncy private education his Mater and Pater had spaffed a chunk of the family fortune on. '…who I'm sure you'll agree, looked absolutely beautiful.'

That drew a round of approving harrumphs from the wedding crowd, punctuated by the occasional tinging of glasses.

'You know, when I started out, all those years ago, I never could have dreamed that I'd be privileged enough to have a *knighthood* conferred upon me by Her Majesty.' The smug git paused for applause, and actually got some.

Not from Roberta, though. She just took another swig of red, and went, 'Wank, wank, wank, wank...' Like a muttering penguin.

'Or to have had the *honour* of serving my country as Under-Secretary of State for Trade and Industry during Sir John Major's time as Prime Minister.'

Assorted hurrahs from the company.

'Ohh look at me being all wanky.'

'That I would have had the *pleasure* of being head of our glorious local Conservative Party.'

Full-on whoops erupted from the crowd.

Another swig of shiraz. 'Glorious bunch of heartless bastards, more like.'

Susan glared at her. 'Robbie!'

'And best of all: to have been your MP for these last thirty years!'

And the crowd goes wild. Cheering. Clapping. Hooting like the bunch of baboons they were.

Ego suitably fed, Sir Just-for-Men finally waved them into silence. 'Of course, I have one more person to thank for their invaluable help in putting this glorious day together.'

Sitting next to him, the mother-of-the-bride preened a bit, getting ready to take all the credit going. She wasn't exactly a spring chicken, but there was still a bit of bite about her. The same strong athletic frame as her daughter, if a little on the plump side. Mind you, that just meant you had more to grab onto between the sheets, didn't it? Bet she went like a jack-hammer when you got her going. Skin that lovely nut-brown colour that only comes with properly exotic holidays.

But Sir Scumbag didn't introduce *her*, instead he gestured down the table to an auld mannie with a military moustache and all his own hair – grey and white, like a badger's ghost. A patrician's air about him, as he sat there in full Highland get-up.

'Ladies and gentlemen, Lord Oliver William Fitzroy-Galbraith.'

Which had to be the Toriest name *of all time.*

The mother-of-the-bride's face sagged at being passed over for Lord Oggildy-Boggildy, but the wedding guests exploded into whoops and cheers again as the old git waved in acknowledgement.

'Who has so *generously* allowed us to use his estate, chapel, and castle, to celebrate Adriana and Douglas's big day.'

Which was a bit rich, given the place was a hotel and had probably cost a fortune to hire. Bet the old git hadn't even given them mates' rates. But then Sir Stinky McHairDye was clearly one of those crawly-bumlick types, who just loved sucking up to the aristocracy.

More hoorahs and hoorays from the other crawly-bumlicks – all of which Lord Fitzroy-Galbraith brushed off with what was probably well-practised modesty.

Roberta topped up her glass and made penguin noises again: 'Wank, wank, wank, wank…'

'So, ladies, gentlemen, and assorted Terrible Trotskyites, please be upstanding and toast the health of our benefactor, Lord Fitzroy-Galbraith!'

Everyone clambered to their feet, glasses raised. Well, everyone except Roberta, because there was no way in a cold and frosty hell that she was toasting another Tory cocknugget. Instead, she stayed sitting, arms folded, muttering yet more penguiny wanks as some anonymous toady launched into a cry of, *'Speech!'*

It was answered by another toady, meaning it had to be mating season for them. *'SPEEEECH!'*

Then they were all at it. A frog chorus of toadies. 'Speech! Speech! Speech! Speech!'

Until, finally, the old git, Lord Thingummy-Whatsit, creaked his way to his feet and hushed them with his hands.

Silence settled across the room, all those eager wee faces turned to the Arch Tory.

He cleared his throat and, in a firm baritone, bestowed upon them the benefit of whatever passed for wisdom with this lot. 'When I first ran for parliament in 1970, it was a sign of great things to come!'

The toadies cheered.

And Roberta folded forward and banged her head off Michael Heseltine.

It was going to be a long, *long* night.

4

Roberta knocked back the last big mouthful of Talisker and thunked the crystal tumbler down on the counter. 'Same again.'

Well, it was a free bar, be rude not to.

And besides, needed something to drown out the pain of being at a Tory wedding.

That wee PC rocked up beside her, stupid shiny-black kilt jacket abandoned somewhere in favour of rolled-up shirtsleeves and a dangly untied bowtie. Handwritten list in one hand, round brown tray in the other. Nothing about him seemed to fit properly, from the kilt to the awkward smile on his scrawny face.

He gave Roberta a nod as the bloke behind the bar placed a fresh tumbler of eighteen-year-old smoky Skye firewater in front of her.

The bartender had the look of an Eastern European turnip magnate, complete with Balkan-style moustache, but the kind of Welsh accent you could open collieries with. He smiled at PC Thin-and-Awkward. 'What can I get for yeow?'

'Hi.' It came out as a high-pitched squeak, so he tried again, reading off his list: 'Hi, can I get a negroni, three gin and tonics – one with cucumber, one with lime, no ice in the other, two merlots, a vesper, a large Balvennie – no water, and I'll have a pint of Tennent's if you've got it?'

'Ooh, sorry, we don't have any Ten-ent's. I can do yeow a Peroni, if that helps?'

The wee lad deflated a bit, but forced his awkward smile back into place again. 'Aye, that'd be great, thanks. Perfect.'

Bet Little Miss Perky-Cleavage walked all over him. And not in a tie-me-up-and-spank-me kind of way.

As the barman went off to get the drinks, Roberta sidled a little closer to PC Doormat. Gave him a good up-and-down – squinting as if really *thinking* about it, before holding up a finger. 'Let me see: callouses on your right hand, that implies some manual work, but there's none on your left… Tan mark around your watch, so you've not been on holiday to get that colour.'

A little pink flush spread across his freckled cheeks. 'Well no, I've—'

'Shhhh!' She waggled the finger at him. Had another squint. 'Mark around your forehead implies you wear a hat. A lot. One with a peak, going by the fact your nose is *slightly* paler than your cheeks.'

His ginger eyebrows went up. Clearly impressed by the performance. 'How did you—'

'You walked up to the bar with a rolling gait. That's someone who's comfortable covering large distances on foot. And, no offence, it looks as if you cut your own hair. Right?'

His mouth hung wide open. 'That's—'

'Police officer.' She narrowed her eyes even further. 'Constable. In…' milking the pause, 'N Division?'

'Wow. That's… You're right!' He positively bounced in place.

She gave him a modest shrug. 'It's a knack that's served me well.' Then dipped into her jacket pocket and pulled out a warrant card. Flipped it open and let him bask in her official Detective-Sergeant-flavoured magnificence.

He stood up straight. 'Detective Chief Inspector?' Actually looked as if he was going to salute. 'Ma'am!'

Wait a minute...

'Detective Chief Inspector?' Roberta turned the warrant card around, and lo and behold, the wee loon was right. According to the card she was still a DCI. Before the big demotion. Suppose, sometimes, honesty was more-or-less the best policy. 'Ah, right, no, it's an old—'

A booming voice cut across the bar. *'Hoy, Mikey!'*

An older man followed it in. Greying, mid-fifties, black-framed glasses. A kilt tight enough to make his belly bulge over the thick leather belt. Like he'd gone to seed a little, but there was still a hint of the man he used to be in the way he moved and held himself. Someone powerful. Hadn't he been on the top table? Yeah: father-of-the-groom, wasn't it?

The new bloke slapped PC Mikey on the back. 'You crushing the grapes for that wine yourself, or what? Taking forever.'

This time the PC's smile was genuine. 'Sarge, this is DCI Steel, she's like some sort of Sherlock Holmes genius!'

The newcomer gave her a once-over. 'You're in the job?'

'Oh aye.'

'Sergeant Sandy Moore.' He stuck out his hand for shaking, a grin splitting his face. 'This calls for a celebration! Mikey, you take them drinks back to the table and I'll keep our senior officer here company. If that's all right, ma'am?'

She backed off a pace, curling her lip. 'You're no' a *Tory*, are you?'

The grin got wider. 'Oh I can see we're going to get on fine!'

You know, Sergeant Sandy Moore was actually OK. For a man. He and Roberta took up positions at the end of the bar, like police-issue gargoyles. Obviously, in Roberta's case, it was a sexy gargoyle, but Sandy fit the bill to a tee. He had a sort of granity cragginess to him. And not just the lines in his face. Like he'd been carved out of sturdy rock for the purpose of locking up wrong 'uns.

Mind you, he was getting kinda pickled.

Couldn't hold his drink as well as she could.

That was men for you.

Roberta's stool was a bit shoogly, so that's why she was wobbling a bit. Nothing to do with the eight or nine or twelve large whiskies they'd had.

Sandy took off his tie and rolled up his sleeves, revealing a thistle tattoo with 'THEY'LL NEVER TAKE OUR FREEDOM!' wrapped around it, as they looked out through the open doorway to the ballroom.

The bride and groom were on display, snog-waltzing their way around the dance floor to a string-quartet version of a Simply Red song. Which just went to show that no amount of money could buy good taste.

Sandy gestured at the groom with his glass. 'Course I wanted the boy to go into policing, but they never listen, do they? Went into local government instead.'

Roberta shook her head. 'Terrible shame.'

'I mean, what's wrong with being a policeman... Officer I mean. No offence, ma'am.'

'They don't know they're born.'

'Now he tells me he's been selected for Aberdeen South – going to be their next Conservative MP if they can beat the SNP.'

'Tragedy.'

Sandy sighed and took a sip of Glen Garioch. 'Don't get me wrong, he's my son and I love him – well, you've got to, don't you? – but a *Tory*...?' He shook his head. 'Do you know they met at the Conservative Party conference? How do you live that down?'

'My heartfelt sympathies.' She patted him on the back. 'You know what'll help? More whisky!'

PC... McKinnon? Think it was McKinnon. Unless it was Mackenzie? No, definitely McKinnon. Anyway, whoever he was, the lad had a nasty habit of going out of focus from time to time, which, let's face it, was just a bit rude.

But he, Sandy, and Roberta all had a Sambuca lined up in front of them, each one topped with flickering purple-and-blue flames. So, she'd overlook it this time.

Roberta slapped a hand down on the bar. 'A toast!'

PC McKinnon raised his burning glass. 'The bride and groom!'

Sandy did the same. 'The bride and groom!'

Ah, what the hell.

She raised her glass too. 'Up your bum!'

Then they blew out the flames and knocked back their drinks. A bit like drinking petrol, but there were worse things at half past eight on a Friday night.

'Waterloo' belted through the open ballroom doors into the bar. Not a weird string-quartet version, the original ABBA one – pounding out of the DJ's speakers, accompanied by flickering yellow, blue, and red lights that pulsed in time with the music.

It was time to face facts: PC McKinnon was definitely drunk. You could tell, because his eyes wouldn't point in the same direction any more and he sort of swayed in his seat more than was appropriate for ABBA. Wobbling away there, on the other side of the table they'd appropriated in the corner of the bar. Definitely drunk.

Probably best drink his whisky for him. You know, for his own good.

'See, the trouble ... the trouble is...' she plucked McKinnon's glass from the tabletop, 'the job's shhhhhagged.' For some reason that last word was slipperier than expected.

Sandy nodded. 'Yup. Shagged. And bug... buggered. Thoroughly shagged and buggered.'

She frowned, then it came to her: 'Shaggered! That's what it is: *completely* shaggered.'

PC McKinnon didn't say anything, just tipped over to one side until a stuffed badger was the only thing keeping him upright. Eyes closed, mouth open, a little trail of drool making its way down his chin.

Sandy took a big gulp of Ardbeg. 'That's ... Police Scotland ... for you. We could've ... could've had the best ... of *all* worlds ... but it all had to be done ... done the *Strathclyde* way, didn't it?'

'Bastards.' She was about to follow that up with a story about the detective sergeant, three gross of pilfered condoms and a stripper called Candy, when 'Waterloo' faded into 'Come on Eileen'. Roberta sank McKinnon's whisky in one. 'Oooh! I love this song! Fall-in, Sergeant.' She lurched to her feet, which took two goes, for some reason. 'We're going dancing!'

The whole bunch of Tory bastards stared at her with horror on their faces as she hauled her hand back and slapped Sir Reginald I'm-a-Massive-Tosser Bradbury-Scott across his fat smug face hard enough to make him crash flat on his arse, right in the middle of the dance floor.

Susan stood there, eyes wide, hands doing that speak-no-evil brass-monkey thing, as 'Back for Good' by Take That wanged out of the DJ's speakers.

Was difficult staying upright, what with the dance floor being all uneven and lurching about like a boat in a storm, but Roberta managed. Keeping one leg moving for balance as she pointed at the lardy git sprawled across the floor. 'Don'… don' you … dare talk to … to my wife … like that!'

Sir Gets-Slapped-a-Lot glowered up at her, rubbing his cheek. 'You, madam, are no lady!'

Right – she was having the bastard.

Roberta lunged for him, but Sandy grabbed her and bundled her away before she could get a decent punch in…

They were in the corner, beside that stupid great-big stag statue, in the lobby. No idea how they got here. Just her and Susan. The two of them against the world.

Well, the world and the line of Tory wedding guests who hadn't booked a room for the night, all boozy and shuffling, heading out through the front doors to the waiting coaches. Banging on about what a splendid day it'd been and what a lovely couple Adriana and Douglas made and wasn't it a shame about that dreadful woman?

No idea who this woman was, but she sounded like a complete nightmare. Getting drunk and picking fights? Who did that at a wedding?

Susan glared at Roberta, hands on her hips, face creased up with angry wrinkles. 'I have *never* been so humiliated in my life! You swore to me you'd behave!'

The carpet in here was even wobblier than that dance floor. Roberta grabbed the statue's plinth for balance. 'C'mon … sss wedding. Juss a little fun, s'all.'

'You're a disgrace!'

Ah, she was just saying that. Playing hard to get.

Roberta puckered up. 'Give's kiss.'

'I can't even *look* at you!' Susan shoved her away, and the whole trying-to-stay-upright thing went for a bumhole.

One minute everything was the right way up, the next Roberta was lying on her back, on the tartan carpet, arms and legs making sad little circles in the air like an upturned turtle. 'Help … I've … I've fallen over … and can' … can' get up!'

But Susan just turned on her heel and stormed off.

No idea how late it was, but the hotel was in darkness as Roberta felt her way along the ballroom wall and through into the bar. Where she helped herself to a half-full bottle of Lagavulin from the rack behind the counter. Removing the cork with her teeth and spitting it away. Swigging a proper-sized mouthful as she staggered out through the conservatory doors and into the night…

Roberta forced her eyes open, but Susan wasn't in the bathroom any more. Not sure if that counted as falling asleep, or passing out. Probably a bit of both.

Grey light oozed in through the net curtains, presumably so no one could see you on the toilet, pooping. Or vomiting your whole innards out.

Now she was awake, the hangover rushed back in like a

surging tide, grabbing her brain and tossing it roughly against the rocky shore. Stuffing it full of angry herring gulls and vicious haddock. But at least there was nothing left to puke up.

That was something, right?

A bright side.

Urgh.

There was an orchestra of bastards trapped inside her skull, doing death-metal covers on bin lids with sledgehammers. And they were crap at it too.

She crawled her way up the towel rail and tottered over to the sink. Stared at the wrinkly horror in the mirror. One side of her face all creased from using the toilet seat as a pillow.

Roberta unbuttoned her vomity shirt and dumped it on the bathroom floor, where it could be all crusty without her, as she filled the sink with cold water and stuck as much of her head as possible under the surface.

Maybe, if she was *really* lucky, she could drown in here.

At least that would make the orchestra stop.

But she surfaced instead, staring at the dripping monstrosity in the mirror. The one in the wrinkly skin and fusty grey bra. The one whose stomach was a measles-dotted mass of itchy midge bites. Then thunked her head against the cool glass. Raised her voice so she could be heard in the other room. 'He was disrespecting you, what was I supposed to do?'

No reply.

One thing you could always rely on Susan for was an industrial-strength sulk.

'He grabbed your backside! If someone grabbed *my* backside you'd deck them, wouldn't you? Bloody hope you would...' Roberta lowered her voice a bit. 'At least, I *think* he grabbed your backside.' She blinked at the bloodshot eyes in the mirror. Had a scratch at the midge bites. 'Maybe it was me?' Nah. Louder again: 'I'm pretty sure it was him!'

She scooped up a double handful of water and sploshed it on her face.

Still nothing from Queen Of The Sulkers, so Roberta dried her face on a fluffy towel and tried to stand up straight again. 'Susan?' Shuffling her way to the door.

The bedroom curtains were open, letting in more insipid sickly light. Rain battered down from the charcoal sky, leaching all colour and life from the world. Or at least the small, misty, soggy bit visible through the window.

'Come on, Susan, don't be like that, I'm hungover I need…'

But Susan wasn't there: the duvet was thrown back, the bed empty, the bedroom door lying wide open. Then a scream slashed its way through Roberta's hangover: distant and terrified.

Susan.

Oh no…

5

'SUSAN!' Roberta sprinted across the bedroom to where a pair of crossed claymores were mounted on the wall above the fireplace, along with a wee round shield. She grabbed the handle of one and yanked. Bloody thing wouldn't move. Some idiot had bolted it up there.

Another scream, from somewhere out in the corridor.

No time to sod about with immovable swords, grab a weapon!

An antique-looking chamber pot sat on the table under the window. It'd have to do.

She snatched it up by the handle and barrelled out into the corridor.

No sign of anyone.

'SUSAN, I'M COMING!'

A man's voice wafted up from the other side of the fire door, loud and trembling: 'There's been a murder!'

Right.

Roberta thumped through the fire door and out onto the balcony that ran along this side of the hotel lobby. A blaze of flickering white crackled through the windows, harsh and bright, and every light in the room went out, plunging the whole place into gloom. Then a deafening roar of thunder, loud enough to make her diaphragm shake.

'SUSAN!'

She battered down the sweeping wooden staircase, barged her way between a fat old git in silk PJs who'd forgotten to put his teeth in and a mouldering debutant smeared with *far* too much night cream. Ran past that stupid statue. 'SUSAN!'

Roberta skittered to a halt on the tartan carpet.

Susan was there, standing in a small group of middle-aged lumpies, everyone in assorted nightclothes with just-clambered-out-of-bed hair. All of them staring up at the huge metal stag that towered above them.

The weird gingery hotel maid was there too, wearing her uniform short tartan skirt and flouncy blouse, clutching her chest and laughing in a kind of *hysterical* manner. Standing with her knees crossed, like she'd wet herself.

Roberta grabbed Susan, pulled her into a one-handed hug, trying not to bash her on the head with the chamber pot. 'Are you all right?'

Susan didn't even look at her. Instead she pointed upwards, still staring at that moronic statue.

OK... Roberta followed the pointy finger.

Wasn't easy to see in the gloom, but there was definitely something up there. The oversized stag had grown some sort of decoration.

Another crackle of lightning threw the lobby into monochrome relief.

Sodding hell.

The 'something up there' was a body, impaled on the stag's metal antlers. Back arched and arms outstretched – the furthermost points poking through the palm of one hand and the wrist on the other arm. As if he'd been crucified. And it was definitely a 'him', because the body's tartan pyjama bottoms were down around his ankles, leaving his shrivelled-up unmentionables on display.

And it was all seared onto Roberta's irises, still visible as the lightning faded, leaving the scene in darkness again. 'Oh, shite.'

This time, when the thunder boomed, it was right on top of them.

It was surprising how much light two dozen smartphones could produce – all of them held up, filming away, getting brighter as more hotel guests shuffled into the lobby to see what the hell all the screaming was about.

Everyone in pyjamas and nighties and fluffy hotel bathrobes. Bleary-eyed and shaggy-haired. Speculating about why and who and how and wasn't it horrible and shocking and grisly and I hope I've got enough battery left to get a good film of it uploaded onto Facebook.

A couple of hotel staff had joined the gathering crowd – that old bloke with the shotgun, in his tweedy outdoors get-up. And the doorman made of string-and-bones, stripped of his kilt but with his knobbly knees still on show, because they poked out from an oversized kitten-pink T-shirt. 'SLEEPYTIME FRIENDS ARE THE BESTEST!' according to the gold sequined letters across its front. The pair of them milling about like they were supposed to do something, but didn't quite know what.

Roberta stared up at the lower naked portions of the dead body. '*Please* tell me that's not who I think it is.'

The redhead maid nodded, her voice full of hushed awe. 'It's Sir Reginald Bradbury-Scott!'

Of course it was. The man she'd tried to slap the smug off, for grabbing Susan's bum. Because Roberta was cursed, wasn't she?

As usual.

She took a deep breath, gave herself a wee shake, and pulled her shoulders back. 'OK, here's what we need to do...'

That old git from the top table marched into the room. Lord Thingummy-Whatsit, the one who'd given the longest and most boring speech known to mankind. The one who owned the place, sweeping in – all imperious, with his paisley-patterned PJs and matching dressing gown. Dramatic entrance complete, he clapped his hands. 'All right, everyone, that's enough. If I can have your attention please?'

But everyone just kept on filming and gossiping.

So, the gamekeeper thumped his shotgun's butt on the floor three times. 'ALL RIGHT, YOU LOT, SILENCE! THE LAIRD'S SPEAKING!'

All those filming phones phones turned to point at the old git in paisley pyjamas.

'Thank you.' Lord Thingumy-BingBong preened a little in the silence. 'Now, I'm sure you're all aware how essential it is we have *order* and *discipline* at times like this, so I'm going to have to ask all the ladies to retire to their rooms. There's no need for you to see any more of this unpleasantness.' He clapped his hands again. 'Off you go, chop, chop. There's good girls.'

Patronising git.

Some of the women did what they were told, which was pretty sodding unbelievable in this day and age. Like feminism never happened. Sir Reginald Bradbury-Scott wasn't the only one in need of a damn hard slap. But before Roberta could do the needful, he was at it again.

'Not to worry, you're all perfectly safe. There we go.' Wafting them away with a dismissive gesture. Trying the same thing with Roberta and Susan. 'You too.'

'Aye, that'll be shining.' She squared up to him, chest and chin out. 'You wanting me to shove my righteous feminist boot up your wrinkly sexist bumhole, grandad?'

He flinched back a couple of steps. 'Your breath is *repulsive*.' Wafting a hand in front of his face. 'And this is a time for level heads, not … undisciplined rude people running around in their revolting underwear.'

Underwear?

Roberta had a wee glance in the downward direction.

Ah. Right. Yup, she'd rushed down here wearing nothing on her top half but her bra. Oh, Old Faithful had *started out* white, but after years and years of washing she'd faded to a kind of dental-plaque-beigey-grey colour. OK, so maybe she wasn't in the first flush of youth, and her underwire had a habit of wandering from time to time, but she was a bra you could *count on*. Dependable. Sturdy. Comfortable. Which was more than could be said of the twin-lacy-black-hammocks monstrosity she'd tried on yesterday.

And at least Roberta's lower half was covered, right? Even if it was in grass-stained suit trousers and damp stripy socks.

Sometimes you just had to work with what you had.

She gave him the benefit of a good hard evil eye. 'Oh, you think so, do you?' Then hauled on her proper DCI voice, the one that struck fear into constables and detective inspectors alike. 'RIGHT, YOU LOT, STOP FILMING THAT BLOODY BODY AND CALL THE POLICE!'

A nervous woman's voice wafted through from the back of the group. 'There's no reception?'

Bit ironic for a wedding…

'Ah yes.' A flat, monotone English accent. 'Storm must've disabled the masts. Happens all the time out here in the sticks.'

A monotone Edinburgh voice joined in. 'And the *power*, of course.' Disappointed tut. 'Surprised somewhere like this doesn't have a backup generator, mind you.'

'That's very true. I know they can be expensive to install, but the support they—'

'Nairn,' the old git in the paisley PJs snapped his fingers, 'see to the generator.'

The gamekeeper actually tugged the brim of his tartan bunnet. 'Aye, Your Lairdship.' Then scurried off, taking his shotgun with him.

The Laird clapped his hands again. 'Now, let's not have any more of this silliness. I'm in command here and—'

'My sharny arse, you are.' Roberta stepped in close, breath and bra be damned. 'I'm—'

'Given your *vulgar* display last night I don't think you're in any position to make demands!'

'Who are you calling "vulgar", you scrotum-faced old bawbag?'

A sneer curled his military moustache. 'You're a nasty woman who *clearly* needs a man's firm hand to teach you humility and some damned manners!'

Right, that was it: time to introduce her knee bone to His Lordship's bollocks as hard as—

Sergeant Sandy Moore pushed his way between them, wearing a pair of Spider-Man pyjamas. And not pyjamas with Spider-Man on them, these were *actually* printed to look like the costume – blue and red, complete with webbing and the logo on his barrel chest. 'All right, break it up!' Forcing them both back, then raising his voice to bellow out: 'CONSTABLE MCKINNON?'

The wee loon's muffled voice came from somewhere over by the ballroom doors. 'Sarge?'

'Get your uniform on. Then: back here ASAP and secure this crime scene!'

'Sarge.'

Sergeant Moore gave Roberta and Lord Thingumy-Whatsit a stern look, then turned to the crowd. 'I need you all to return to your rooms and stay there until you're called on for a statement.' Another stern look. 'And that's *all* of you, not just the ladies.'

His Lordship straightened up to his full height. 'I think you'll find that *I'm* the ranking official here, Sergeant. And it's *my* castle, so I'll—'

'With all due respect, Lord Fitzroy-Galbraith, the ranking official is right there.' Moore pointed at her. 'Detective Chief Inspector Roberta Steel, NE Division.'

Oops… He still thought she was a DCI.

Should really have said something about that.

Kinda too late, now.

Susan had a bit of a glare at her. Not sure if that was a 'You're not a DCI any more!' glare, or a 'You're embarrassing me in your ancient bra!' glare, or even a 'You got blootered last night and acted like a proper arsehole!' one. Some days were just an embarrassment of riches.

That boring Edinburgh drone started up again. 'Ah, yes, but this is *Highlands and Islands* Division, isn't it? So, I think you'll find a DCI from Northeast Division doesn't have jurisdiction here.'

His drony English friend joined in. 'He makes a very good point.'

'Oh, thank you.' Smug git.

Sergeant Moore held up a hand. 'Under Police Scotland, she has jurisdiction *everywhere*.'

There was some grumbling at that, but nothing more from the Boring Brothers.

Roberta nodded. 'All right, you heard the sergeant: back to your rooms the lot of you.'

No one moved.

'Go on, shoo!'

It earned her some dark looks, but finally the wedding guests and hotel staff got the message and drifted away, disappearing upstairs – leaving the lobby empty, except for Roberta, Susan, Sergeant Moore, and Lord Fitzroy-Galbraith. And the body, of course.

Lordy glowered down his nose at her. 'Don't think you've heard the last of this. I'm *very* good friends with the Chief Constable!'

'Aye, good for you.' Roberta gave him a wee wink. 'You can have a nice whinge when the pair of you are rolling up your trouser legs in the Lodge next time. Till then...' She clapped her hands, just like he had, not even trying to hide the grin on her face. 'Chop, chop, off you trot. There's a good boy.'

A haughty sniff, then His Lordship turned smartly on his heel and marched off in proper parade-ground style. Back straight, arms swinging.

The effect was somewhat undermined by the PJs and dressing gown, though.

Soon as the old prick had gone she let everything slump. 'Urrrrgh...' Massaging her temples with a shaky hand. 'My head...'

For some unfathomable reason, Susan didn't come through with tea and sympathy. 'Serves you right for drinking all that whisky last night; you should know better at your age! And why aren't you wearing a top? Bad enough *I* have to suffer your horrid grey bra, does everyone else need to see it?'

Fine, well two could play at that game. Especially if she was going to be nasty about Old Faithful.

Roberta jerked a thumb in Susan's direction. 'Sergeant?'

Took him a moment, but he got there in the end. 'Ah, right.' Moore guided Susan towards the stairs. 'If you don't mind, madam, this is a police matter, now. Thank you for your co-operation.'

A puzzled frown. 'But I'm—'

He gave her a gentle shove. 'Thank you, that's a great help. Off you go.'

Susan stopped at the foot of the stairs and looked back at Roberta.

Yeah, not going to happen.

Then Susan gave a pointed, 'Humph!' and marched off.

Probably going to pay for that later, but what could you do?

Roberta slumped against the reception desk and buried her face in her hands, trying to squeeze the burning weasels back inside her skull.

Sergeant Moore's voice happied its way through her weasel wrangling. 'I've wanted to do that for *years*. Pull rank on the old bugger: put him in his place!' He launched into a less than flattering impersonation for, '"I'm Lord *Fitzroy-Galbraith* and *I'm* on the 1922 committee, *I* brought down Theresa May, I'm *much* more important than you lowly police plebs!"'

When Roberta peered out between her fingers, Moore was making wanking gestures.

A laugh. 'Important *this*, Your Lordship.' He frowned at her. 'Are you OK?'

'No.'

'Ah, OK.' He took a couple of steps back and stared up at the body. 'Never done a murder before. Couple of missing persons and the occasional domestic, but drink driving's the crime *à la mode d' ici*.'

PC McKinnon scurried back into the lobby, fiddling with the Velcro on his stabproof vest. He'd changed into the full Police Scotland kit, peaked cap just a little bit too large for him, making the tips of his ears stick out at right angles. 'What did I miss?'

'Just said I've never done a murder before.'

'Oh, aye.' He followed the sergeant's gaze up to Sir Reginald Bradbury-Scott and his exposed nether regions. 'Could be suicide, though. Or an accident?'

'Very true. Have to keep an open mind with something like this.'

Idiots.

Roberta groaned. Gave her forehead another squeeze. 'Coffee...'

PC McKinnon pulled a face. 'Knowing our luck, it's probably an accident, though.'

A sigh. 'More than likely, but a boy can dream.'

OK, they were clearly not listening, so she tried again. 'Coffee!'

Sergeant Moore shook his head. 'Don't think that's—'

'Coffee, coffee, coffee!'

'It's just: the power's out.'

Of course it was. The lightning had fried something important and now there wasn't any electricity. No electricity, no kettle. No kettle, no boiling water. No boiling water, no coffee!

'Noooooo...' She slumped even further into her *completely* undeserved misery. Then scowled at both of them. 'You're a pair of idiots, you know that, don't you?'

'Hey!' Moore looked a bit hurt at that. 'It's not our fault the power's—'

'How the hell is this an accident? Look at it.'

They did.

And then, after an awkward silence, PC McKinnon raised one shoulder in a half-arsed shrug. 'I don't get it.'

How did this pair ever get to be police officers?

She held up a hand, counting the points off on her fingers, rudest digits first. 'One: how do you *accidentally* slip and fall on a massive great metal stag statue? It's no' like he was hoovering naked, is it? And it's, what, sixteen, eighteen feet from down here to those antlers?'

'Well, maybe he was—'

'And where's he going to fall from?'

A pause as they looked at the body, then at the stairs behind it, and the balconies on either side of the lobby. The only thing *in front* of the statue was the castle wall – adorned with a couple of dangly woven banners, depicting hunting scenes, that looked in need of a good wash. And possibly burning.

She pointed. 'Come on then, Hamish Macbeth, was he shinning up a tapestry and lost his grip?'

Pink rushed up Sergeant Moore's cheeks. 'Ah...'

'Then let's take a look at the *main* impediment to this so called "theory".' Her index finger joined the middle one. 'Two: what happens when you slip and fall on a dirty-big set of pointy metal antlers?'

PC McKinnon had a go at that one: keen, but dim. 'You die?'

'You *bleed*, you corrugated funtmuppet. And are we currently standing in a humongous pool of blood? Anyone?'

Moore groaned as common sense finally worked its way through his six-inch-cavity-wall-insulated cranium. 'He was already dead when he went up there!'

'Give that man a Bounty Bar! There's hope for you yet, Sandy. Only way you'd get a body up there would be a ladder. And a really long one at that.'

'Ooh, ooh,' McKinnon bounced up and down, 'so maybe the pyjamas round the ankles is, like, a *message*!'

'Something sexual?' Moore's face creased. 'Or maybe it's a ritual humiliation?'

'Or maybe his breeks fell down when he was chucked there.'

The three of them stared up at Sir Reginald Bradbury-Scott's half-naked remains.

One thing was certain: whatever the message *was*, someone had gone to a lot of trouble sending it.

6

Roberta sniffed – scrunching up one side of her face as the orchestra in her cranium abandoned death metal for acid jazz. 'You *sure* there's no coffee? My head's like a booby-trapped litter tray.'

Sergeant Moore gave her an appraising once-over. 'Speaking of booby traps: Mikey, give the DCI your high-vis, eh?'

'Oh. Right. Sorry.' He peeled the high-vis waistcoat from his stabproof vest and held it out to her. 'Might smell a bit of sheep…'

'Bloody hell…' He wasn't kidding – the thing was rank, like someone had marinated a Yorkshire terrier in dung and fusty ditch-water. But it was better than nothing, so she pulled it on and fastened it up. Stinky thing was about three sizes too big, but it covered a multitude of sins. Not very well, though. Could still see a chunk of Old Faithful, in all her baggy grey glory, through the gaps.

'Better.' Moore slapped PC McKinnon on the shoulder. 'Now, go get the crime-scene kit from the Landy. I want this whole area cordoned off. Just like we practised.'

'Sarge.'

He was halfway to the door when Roberta grabbed him and wrestled his Airwave handset out of its mount on his stabproof vest.

She clicked the button. 'Alpha Bravo Six Niner to Control, need urgent assistance at Skirivour Castle.'

But when she let go of the button the only response was a hissing crackle from the handset's speaker.

'Alpha Bravo Six Niner to Control, do you read me, over?'

'Sorry.' The constable gave her an uncomfortable smile. 'Tried it when I got back to the room. It works off the same towers as the mobile phone signal.'

'Sod.' She tossed the handset back to McKinnon.

He grabbed for it, fumbled the catch, and just barely managed to stop it crashing down on the tartan carpet. Then scrambled away, out through the front doors and into the rain.

Useless lump.

'Bet there's *one* thing no one's tried.' She lumbered over to the reception desk. The phone was one of those beige pushbutton monstrosities that acted like a mini switchboard. Roberta put the handset to her ear and poked the button marked, 'OUTSIDE LINE'.

Not so much as a dialling tone.

She poked the Outside Line button a couple more times, just to make sure.

Sergeant Moore shook his head. 'We're at the end of a branch of a branch of a spur of another branch. Every time we get a proper storm, lightning hits the wires and blows our poor creaky wee exchange.'

Roberta thumped the handset back into its cradle. 'Cock.'

'Be lucky if they've got it fixed by this time next month.'

Every single sodding thing had to go wrong, didn't it?

She marched off a couple of paces, turned and marched back again. 'OK, so we can't call for backup or Scene Examiners... What about driving to the nearest station and rounding up all the local bunnets?'

'There's only me and Mikey covering an area the size of

Luxembourg. Well, maybe not *Luxembourg*, but definitely two or three Liechtensteins.'

She stared at him.

A shrug. 'Went there on holiday last year.'

'Did your mum drop you on your...'

There was a weird metallic, *'ping, ping, ping,'* noise and the lobby lights flickered on again. Tweedy the gamekeeper must've got the backup generator working.

Couldn't help grinning at that. 'Ya wee beauty!'

Sergeant Moore nodded. 'You thinking what I'm thinking?'

'Oh, yes.'

Even with the lights on, the hotel kitchen was a gloomy wee hole. The kind of place where they clearly didn't believe in windows, opting for lots of stainless steel instead, with dark-red tiles on the floor. A bit like being stuck in a robot's rectum.

Roberta curled forward over a countertop, resting her cheek against the cool metal while the kettle rattled to a boil.

Sergeant Moore placed two mugs in front of the kettle and followed them up with a jar of instant coffee. 'For the record, this is *not* what I was thinking.'

She squinted at him. 'And would it kill you to knock up a bacon roll? Starving here...'

'We need to talk about something.'

'Wonder if there's any leftovers in the fridge?' Roberta scuffed over to the walk-in refrigerator, set into the back wall, by a big rack of pots and pans. Clunked open the door.

A rush of cool air slumped out to meet her, wrapping its chilly arms around her body, setting a wave of goose bumps rippling along her bare arms. Lovely.

Inside, the fridge was full of metal racks, all stacked high with boxes of vegetables and meat and whatnot. She stepped inside and the internal fan kicked in, whirring away as she stalked her way along the lines of shelving. Breath misting around her head, like a lungful of vape.

Out in the kitchen, Sergeant Moore's voice took on a 'breaking bad news' kind of tone, doing its best to sound tactful as it wafted into the fridge. *'Our victim, Sir Reginald, father-of-the-bride…'*

'What about him?'

'You assaulted him last night.'

Oh…

'I didn't "assault" him, we had a fair and frank exchange of views, that's all.' A bunch of industrial-strength Tupperware boxes took up the shelving rack at the end of the fridge. She grabbed one at random and creaked off the lid. Leftover roast potatoes. Not bad.

'Only, you know, that puts you on the list of suspects.'

'Suspects smushpects.' She creaked the lid off another box: carrots and peas, all mixed together like a DIY vomit kit. 'Urgh.' The lid went on again and the Tupperware got stuffed back where it came from. 'Scotland would be a better place if more people gave the landed gentry a damn hard slap every now and then.'

Next box: roast beef – still nice and pink. Result.

Roberta grabbed it. 'And he fondled my wife's arse. What would *you* do?'

There was another smaller box, and when she got the top off, the rich brown scent of gravy oozed out. Looked terrible – all flobby and jellified – but it probably tasted great.

'The optics aren't great, him turning up dead like that, is all I'm saying.'

She stacked it, and the beef, on top of the Tupperware

full of roast tatties and carried them back through into the kitchen. Thumping the fridge door shut behind her.

Sergeant Moore was waiting, face all creased and serious, arms folded. Strict.

Roberta dumped her pilfered food on the countertop and pointed over at the other wall. 'See if there's any bread in that bread bin.'

He sighed, then wandered over there, taking his serious face with him. 'You *didn't* kill him, did you?'

'*Moi?*'

He plonked a loaf of sliced white down in front of her. 'Only if you did, now would be the time to say. I wouldn't even blame you.'

She wrestled the lids off the tatties, gravy, and beef. 'Is that your interviewing technique? Cos it needs work.' Next up, the loaf – slapping a couple of slices straight onto the countertop. Roberta dug a knife into the congealed gravy and slathered both bits of bread with it.

'Yes, but you didn't *actually* kill him?'

Cheeky sod.

'Course I didn't.' She plucked a cold roast potato from its box and crushed it between two fingers, like it was one of Lord Fitzroy-Galbraith's testicles. Stuck the squashed tattie on the gravy-buttered bread and followed it with a few more. Did the same with the other slice. 'And do you know *how* you know that I'm telling the truth? They wouldn't have found his body if I had. No' even teeny-weeny bits of it.'

It wasn't really the right knife for the job, but Roberta used it to hack ragged slices off the roast beef anyway, laying them onto both layers of crushed roasties. 'Aye, and it's two and a coo in that coffee, by the way.'

Last up: she butter-gravied two more slices of white and flopped them down on top of the two sandwiches. OK, so they weren't going to win Celebrity MasterChef anytime soon, but it was the thought that counted.

Sergeant Moore put a mug of coffee in front of her. Eyes narrowed, watching as she sawed each sandwich in half. 'Milk, two sugars.' He followed the mug with a blister pack of pills. 'Found those too.'

'Paracetamol? Oh, you wee dancer.' She clicked half a dozen out into her palm and washed them down with a swig of too-hot coffee. Sighed. Smiled. Then pushed one of her monster sandwiches in his direction. 'Get that down you.' Ripping out a giant bite of her own one – all slithery and meaty and chewy and potatoey too. Talking around the delicious mouthful. 'Mggnnnph mmmnmmmt gnnnphhnnnng mmmmmphnnt?'

Cheeky sod had the brass neck to look at the sandwich she'd so *kindly* made for him like she'd just plopped a handful of cat turds between two slices of bread without even the benefit of mayonnaise.

She swallowed her mouthful. 'Clean your lugs out: how many people stayed over after the wedding?'

'Oh. About forty? It's not that big a hotel.'

Sod. That was still a lot of potential suspects.

'What about staff?'

He frowned for a bit, then, 'Can't be more than a dozen?'

So, even more potentially guilty buggers. 'Eat your RBT-and-G.'

He took a teeny wee bite, like the contents were going to kill him.

Roberta frowned at her sandwich. 'So, that's fifty-two people needing interviewed. Call it a half hour each, that's...' Nope, hangover brain was not cooperating.

'Twenty-six hours?'

'Aye. Twenty-six hours – it'd take us all buggering weekend.

With no proper interview room, no downstream monitoring suite, no recording equipment. And it's no' like we can do PNC checks on them first, is it? Be going at it blind...' She drummed her fingers on the countertop. 'Nah: we'll just have to hold the fort till N Division get a Major Inquiry Team up here. Keep everyone on lockdown.' More drumming. '*Mind you*, we don't want to look like we've just been sat on our thumbs, do we?'

Sergeant Moore took another, bigger bite, getting gravy on his chin. 'Actually, this isn't half bad. Needs a bit of mustard, though.'

As he went a-rummaging, Roberta did the hard job of working out the logistics:

'Fifty-two suspects, less the corpse, and *I* didn't kill him, so call it fifty ... carry the two ... that makes it sixteen-and--two-thirds each. Mind you, how do you spot a deranged, heartless, amoral psychopath when everyone's a *Tory*? Like trying to spot a Mars Bar in a swimming pool full of jobbies.'

He emerged from a cupboard holding a wee yellow jar aloft. 'English mustard!'

'Maybe we can thin the herd a bit? Must be some of them who didn't hate Sir Reginald's slimy bum-grabbing guts.'

'Don't look at me.' Sergeant Moore got himself a clean knife and spread one side of his soggy gravied-bread with a thin scraping of hot yellow mustard, then passed the jar over.

'OK, what do we know about our victim?' Roberta didn't go in for any of this namby-pamby thin scraping nonsense. The whole point of mustard was to slather the stuff on, like Nutella on Keira Knightley's buttocks.

He shuddered watching her. 'Got his knighthood in 1991, "services to charity and local politics" for which you can read "making a scandal involving a high-ranking cabinet member and a Lithuanian rent boy go away". Been the local MP here for yonks. Weighed in on a handful of dodgy planning decisions. Made a fortune in privatised healthcare and some,' Moore made a set of air quotes with his gravy-greased fingers, '"completely above board" property deals. Married: two kids, one's an investment banker, and the other's now my daughter-in-law. Because apparently I did something horrible in a former life.'

More than likely.

She chewed her way through a spicy mouthful, getting the full-on eye-and-nose-watering mustard hit. 'Property deals are a good place to start: plenty of motive when there's cash involved.'

'Had his fingers in a ski resort that never managed to turn a profit, despite being jam-packed every year; a leisure centre in Dundee that "accidentally" burned down; and a bunch of flats in Edinburgh – chucked up when they were building the parliament,' more air quotes, '"allegedly" used to launder money from his vodka-swilling mates in the Kremlin. Some dodgy "investment opportunities". Bunch of other stuff, but most of it seems legit.'

Roberta raised an eyebrow. 'You been keeping tabs on him?'

'Soon as I found out he was going to be family? Aye.'

They slurped and chewed in silence for a bit.

Why did it feel like they were missing something? Something they should've done already? Something important...?

Oh, buggering hell. Of course: 'Anybody told the next of kin yet?'

Sergeant Moore slumped. 'Lady Bradbury-Scott... Didn't see her in the lobby.'

'Finish your sarnie, we've got a death message to deliver.'

This part of the castle was just that bit swankier than the one Roberta and Susan were staying in. The wallpaper just that bit more lush. The shade of red it was painted, just that bit more affluent. The carpet just that bit deeper in its tartany pile.

Polished oak wainscoting on the walls. Yet more stuffed animals in display cases.

The door at the end was named, 'MACALLAN VALERIO ADAMI 1926'. So, just that bit wankier too.

Roberta gave Sergeant Moore a poke. 'Well, don't just stand there, knock!'

'Yes, ma'am.' He had a go, but it was pretty crap to be honest. Two gentle raps on the varnished wood. Followed by an awkward silence.

She checked her watch – quarter to seven. What a way to start someone's day...

Rain drummed against the window.

Outside, wind howled through the trees.

Sergeant Moore shuffled his feet.

Oh, for God's sake.

She gave him another poke. 'Do it again! Only better.'

At least this time the door got a proper police-officer knock – three, hard and sharp.

He cleared his throat. 'Mikey ... PC McKinnon, told me about your deduction thing. You know, figuring out he was Job, just by looking at him?'

Quarter to seven, so where was the widow?

'Thought Sir Reginald's wife was meant to be in?'

'No, but how did you *do* that? How did you know he was Job?'

She gave the door a good battering. 'POLICE! OPEN UP, OR WE'LL HAVE TO FORCE ENTRY!'

His face went a shade of shaky grey. 'I don't think we can just...'

She tried the handle – it turned. Not locked. Fair enough.

Roberta opened the door and stepped inside. 'Come on, then.'

'... or maybe we can.'

It was a sitting room, the kind of place estate agents called 'well appointed', 'spacious', and 'boldly decorated', with lots of velvet curtains and the obligatory tartan carpet, tartan cushions, and a tartan three-piece suite too.

The curtains were open, letting in that thin rainy light. Good view, though: down an avenue of oak trees, to the lochan at the bottom. All of it whipped by the wind and crackling rain.

Lightning flashed in the distance, followed a few seconds later by another roll of thunder.

A couple of doors led off the room, one on either side.

Roberta ran a finger along the dust-free top of a sideboard – where a platter of fruit was displayed next to an unopened bottle of Veuve Clicquot in an ice-free ice bucket. 'All right for some, isn't it?'

She tried the nearest door.

A HUGE bathroom lurked on the other side. A large roll-top bath sat in the middle of it, surrounded by weird pipes and nozzles and taps, as if the hotel had got Heath Robinson blootered on mescal and asked him to design a shower. Fancy tiles on the floor and walls, lovely view of the rain-lashed estate from the window. Even had a bidet, because who didn't love a clean bumhole?

She closed the door and tried the other one, while Sergeant Moore just stood there fidgeting, like someone had filled his Spider-Man PJs with burning ants.

The curtains were drawn, but just enough light oozed in around their edges to make out a gargantuan canopied bed, antique furniture, and a Corby trouser press. *Très* swanky.

A woman lay on her back, on top of the duvet, wearing a

silky nightdress and a frilly eye-mask. Grey hair all wrapped up in curlers. Arms crossed over her chest. Clearly going for the Bride-of-Dracula look. Or, in this case, Mother-of-the-Bride-of-Dracula.

An expensive Rolex-looking watch sat on the nightstand beside her, a matching white stripe on her right wrist cutting through the exotic tan to show where it usually lived.

Lady Bradbury-Scott.

Roberta sniffed. 'Bleeding heck, smells like a tart's knicker drawer in here.' She edged towards the bed. 'Hello?'

Nothing from Dracula's mother-in-law.

Sergeant Moore shuffled his feet again. 'She's not dead too, is she?'

'Don't be so damp.' Roberta inched closer to the bed. 'Wakey, wakey?'

'Oh, Lord, she's dead as well.' He paced up and down at the end of the four-poster. 'It's a disaster…'

'Will you shut up?'

'We've got a serial killer, roaming the castle, picking off the landed gentry!'

7

Roberta reached out and put a hand on Lady Bradbury-Scott's leg. Gave it a wee shake. 'Hello?'

'See! She's dead. And you know who they're going to blame, don't you?'

Two corpses in one day...

Roberta moved further up the body, till she was standing next to its head. Was bad enough when a wedding featured a drunken punch-up, never mind a pair of murders. That said, there didn't seem to be a mark on her, so maybe this was your basic murder-suicide pact? Lady Bradbury-Scott catches her husband, the scumbag, pinching other people's wives' arses and does away with him, impales him on the big stag, and comes back here to overdose on whatever pills she's got packed in her toilet bag.

OK. Well, better check anyway. Duty of care to the public, and all that.

Mind you, feeling for a pulse was always a tricky one.

So, how about... Roberta reached out, took hold of the lace-edged sleeping mask and pulled the whole thing upward till the elastic was stretched tight, then let it ping back down again.

Lady Bradbury-Scott sat bolt upright and screamed.

Roberta screamed too, leaping away from the bed.

Sergeant Moore did the same thing, clutching at his chest,

eyes like oversized pickled onions. 'AAAAAAAAAAAAAAA-AAAAAARGH!'

Lady Screamsalot ripped off the sleeping mask. 'WHO THE HELL ARE YOU? WHAT ARE YOU DOING IN MY BEDROOM? WHERE'S MY HUSBAND?'

Roberta held up her hands. 'Police! We're the police!'

'HELP! POLICE! I'M BEING ASSAULTED BY PERVERTS!'

'WE *ARE* THE POLICE, YOU DAFT DEAF BINT! Now, could we tone the volume down while we've all still got our eardrums?'

A frown. 'WHAT?' Then she pulled out a set of earplugs, scrabbled a hand across the nightstand and put on her glasses. Frowned at the man standing at the bottom of her bed. 'Sandy? What are you doing here?'

He looked down at his Spider-Man PJs, then at Roberta. Who took a quick peek at her own baggy high-vis waistcoat that, to be completely honest, didn't really complement the ancient grey bra underneath.

Let's face it: they *probably* didn't look the picture of a modern, responsible police force.

'Well?'

Sergeant Moore sat on the bed, next to Lady Bradbury-Scott, and took her hand. Swallowed. Licked his lips. Took a deep breath. 'I'm sorry, Jocasta, but we've got some very bad news...'

Roberta hauled a clean T-shirt on over Old Faithful, and tucked it into her jeans. Checked her reflection in the mirror: 'ASK ME ABOUT MY RADICAL LESBIAN FEMINIST AGENDA' in bold white capitals on a dark-pink background.

And, maybe, with a wee bit of slap on, she wouldn't look like she'd dropped out the back end of Mr Rumpole any more. Well, maybe a *little* bit, but there was nothing wrong with lying to yourself every now and then.

Susan glowered at her from the chair by the rain-rattled window – the expression on her face well suited to a wet weekend. 'I don't see why *I* have to be cooped up in here all day, it's not as if *I* killed him!'

Oh, this hotel room was just one gigantic ball of warmth and love, wasn't it?

'It's a murder investigation, OK? Everyone's confined to barracks.' Roberta wandered through into the bathroom and toothpasted her toothbrush. Stuffed it in her gob for a good hard scrub, overflowing with minty froth as Susan's voice stabbed through from the bedroom.

'"Oh, I've come all the way out here to surprise you!" you said. "We'll have a nice romantic break!" you said. And now you're working *again*.'

Wasn't easy, making yourself heard with a mouthful of toothpaste foam, but she had a bash: 'Well, what am I supposed to do? You've seen what passes for the local plod here: the Chuckle Brothers would be more use, and one of them's dead.' More scrubbing. 'Besides, I'm ranking officer.'

'*You're a detective* sergeant, *not a detective chief inspector!*'

Time for the molars. 'No' my fault there was an old warrant card in my jacket, was it? I've no' had that thing on for years.'

'*You shouldn't have told them—*'

'I didn't! That would be what we in the police call "very, very naughty."' Spit. Sploosh a bit of water on the old face to wash away all the foamy white. How did one wee worm of toothpaste create this much mess? Should be able to brush your teeth without looking like you'd just starred in a mint-flavoured bukkake video. 'All I'm doing is holding the fort till the cavalry gets here. After that, we can sod off home.'

'But—'

'Or go somewhere "romantic". You pick. Long as it's no' pishing with rain and I can look at hotties in their bikinis all day.' Roberta scrubbed her face with one of those lovely fluffy hotel towels. Grabbed her leather jacket on the way out. 'Now, if you'll excuse me, I've got two numpties to supervise and a killer to catch.'

While she'd been upstairs getting changed, the Crime Scene Fairies had paid the lobby a visit, festooning it with streamers of not-so-festive bunting. The blue-and-white kind with, 'POLICE' on it.

Roberta, Sergeant Moore, and PC McKinnon stood inside the cordon, looking up at Sir Reginald Bradbury-Scott in all his half-naked-and-deadness.

She wasn't the only one who'd taken the opportunity to change – Sergeant Moore no longer looked as if he could do whatever a spider could, going for the kind of casual-trousers-and-a-polo-shirt combo that probably went down great guns at the local golf club.

He sucked on his teeth for a bit. Then, 'We can't just *leave* him there. He's the local MP, it's undignified.'

'Aye…' PC McKinnon pulled a face. 'But the crime-scene management handbook clearly states that "all remains are to be examined in situ by the appropriate professionals and all efforts taken to preserve the scene."'

'His *willy's* hanging out, Mikey.'

'I didn't write the manual.'

Sergeant Moore threw his hands out. 'And we can't keep people confined to their rooms forever! Going to have a riot on our hands if it goes past lunchtime. They'll all need fed and watered.'

Which was true, but then again, they were all Tories, so sod them.

Roberta shook her head. 'The wee loon's right: no mucking about with the crime scene.'

That didn't stop Moore whinging on about it, though. 'What's the temperature meant to hit today, Mikey? Twenty-three, twenty-four degrees?'

McKinnon checked his phone. Frowned at the lack of signal, because he wasn't the sharpest. A shrug. 'Twenty-seven?'

'Aye, and that's with sky-high humidity as well. We leave Sir Reginald up there in that heat and you can cut the flies with a spoon. Whole place will be thick with them.'

'Aye, but the manual—'

'Heat and insects are gonna degrade our forensic evidence, till—'

'Hoy!' Roberta gave them both a good hard stare. '*No one* touches that body till the pathologist gets here. And that's final. We're no' screwing this one up before the investigation's even started, understand?'

No reply, so she gave Sergeant Moore a good hard poke, too. 'Understand?'

He sighed. Nodded. 'Yes, ma'am.'

'Good boy. Start drawing up a list of everyone in the place. We'll need to interrogate the whole sodding lot when I get back.' She snapped her fingers and marched for the front doors. 'Constable: heel!'

McKinnon did what he was told, leaving Sergeant Moore standing beneath their half-naked knight of the realm.

'But ...' Moore shuffled his feet, 'where are you going?'

She hauled the door open. 'Me and your wee loon need to see a man about some backup.'

Which would have been a really cool line to exit on, if McKinnon hadn't got tangled up in his own feet and stumbled into the door, thumping it closed again before she could escape.

Idiot.

'Sorry...' He pulled it open and held it for her.

She stepped out, under that big portico. Its soggy red-white-and-blue bunting flapped in the wind as rain battered down, sparking in the fountain's bowl. Strafing the puddles that stretched across the gravel driveway. Hissing and growling in the trees.

No sign of the gold balloons. Maybe—

A flicker of white forced back the gloom, followed by a thunderous roar.

Oh yeah, this was going to be lovely.

Roberta nipped inside again and grabbed an umbrella from the stand beside the door.

By the time she got back outside, PC McKinnon was standing at the edge of the portico – grimacing out at the rain. 'We're going to get absolutely soaked, aren't we?'

'Speak for yourself.' She popped the brolly open, revealing a large blue canopy with 'SKIRIVOUR CASTLE HOTEL' in gold letters.

The cheeky wee sod eased himself up next to her, snuggling in under the umbrella. 'I'm in the overflow car park.'

Of course he was.

The overflow car park was doing exactly what the name implied. Vast ocean-sized puddles shimmered as rain bounced off the roofs and bonnets of the assembled fancy vehicles.

Porsches, Ferraris, Audis, more Range Rovers and Jaguars than you could shake a soggy umbrella at.

The police Land Rover stood out like a tramp at the ballet. The thing was filthy, clarted in mud so thick even the current monsoon couldn't shift it. Dents and scrapes down both sides. A crack in the windscreen. It wasn't even one of the new ones; damn thing looked as if it'd been built out of rusty Lego, with a winch on the front and a snorkel exhaust.

And the idiot McKinnon had parked it so far away that Roberta's shoes were squelchy waterlogged horrors by the time they got there.

Soon as he plipped the locks, she scrambled inside. Where it was every bit as manky as the outside. Only, what was that *smell*? Like a million wet dogs had rolled around in fox shit.

'*Stinks* in here. When did you last clean this tip?'

McKinnon clambered in and clunked his door shut. 'I spent most of yesterday rescuing soggy sheep.'

'Aye, well I hope "rescuing" isn't you back-wood bunnets' way of saying "having sexual relations with".'

The engine coughed and spluttered into life – momentarily drowned out by another booming roar of thunder as rain pinged off the Land Rover's roof.

'Should we not do a risk assessment before we head out? I mean, with the weather and everything?'

She shoogled the water off her brolly and into the filthy footwell. 'Don't be so wet. Foot down, Constable Sheep-Shagger.'

Instead, he gazed out through the windscreen. Looking pained as wind rattled the treetops and rain pummelled the overflow car park, beneath a glowering sky the colour of coal. 'All right, but I want it on record that—'

'Blah, blah, blah. Less moaning, more driving.'

One last grimace, then he put the Land Rover in gear and sploshed through the puddles and out of the car park.

If anything, the trees lining the road looked even angrier than the ones around the hotel, branches whipping back and forth as the downpour howled at them.

Roberta cranked up the blowers and the scent of burning dust joined the general sheepiness. She plonked her soggy feet on the dashboard. 'You ever run into this Sir Rodney Bad-Bogey-Snott?'

'Sir Reginald Bradbury-Scott.' There was a pause and a frown. 'He's a man of ... very strong opinions. Or at least, he was.'

'Ah, you mean he was a dick.'

'Liked to throw his title about. You know the type: favours for the lads, best friends with the Chief Constable, that kind of thing.'

'Like our mate, Lord Misogyny-Gitbag the third.'

McKinnon pursed his lips and sighed. 'Two worms in a rotten apple, that pair.' The Land Rover wheeched around a bend and through a huge puddle, sending arcs of water splashing into the rhododendron bushes on either side of the road. 'Course, Sir Reginald really burned his bridges with his "surefire", "can't fail" investment thing. Lot of local families got screwed on that one.'

'Oh aye?' Roberta flexed her soggy toes in her sodden shoes, sending foot-water squishing out through the lace holes to trickle down the dashboard. 'What investment thing is this then?'

'My mum and dad nearly lost their house over it.' He curled his lip, like he'd got a pube stuck between his teeth. 'Thought they were going to make a fortune. A *literal* goldmine, right here in Skirivour Glen. Wasn't a single household didn't sink a big chunk of money into it.' He gave a bitter little laugh. 'Daft, really. You know that old doodah about "if something looks too good to be true"?'

'Hmmm...' Bankrupting the local community wasn't a bad motive for murder. Which meant they'd have to interview all the inbred yokels out here in banjo country – had to be at least *one* of them with access to the hotel last night and a good reason to kill the swindling dickhead.

She had a wee scratch at Old Faithful. 'What about sexy stuff?'

'Kinks and perversions, you mean?' A shrug. 'Probably liked to be spanked and wear nappies, but that's members of parliament for you, isn't it?'

Lightning ripped across the charcoal sky, strobe-lighting the waterlogged road. The bellow of thunder that followed was loud enough to make the whole Land Rover shake.

McKinnon tightened his grip on the wheel, making his knuckles stand out as a wee nervous laugh squeaked free. 'That was close!'

Wimp.

'Come on then: affairs. Was he humping anyone behind their large, beefy, vengeful husband's back? Bet an arse-grabbing tosser like Sir Reginald Bumwanky-Shite was at it with every woman in the place.'

'Oh *definitely*. I heard he keeps a mistress in Inverness and another in Plockton.'

'Hmm...' Roberta frowned out the window, watching the sagging trees whip past. 'I know it's a pretty place, but it always sounds like a venereal disease to me. *Plockton.*' She put on her best doctor's voice for, 'I'm sorry, Mrs McGinty, but you've got a nasty dose of the Plocktons, we're going to have to amputate your bits.'

The Land Rover rocked down and up again as it charged through a puddle deep enough to send water swooshing the bonnet, the windscreen wipers struggling to cope with the deluge of muddy water. Smearing the dirt about.

'Think he had a fling with his PA, but she got married to some party bigwig and moved to Edinburgh.' McKinnon turned the steering wheel, taking them around a hard right, leaning forward in his seat to peer through the filthy windscreen. 'Then there's the local ladies! He was— AAAAAAA-AAAAAAAAAAAAAAAAAAARGH!' Eyes wide, death-grip on the steering wheel, both legs stiff out in front of him as he slammed on the brakes.

8

The ABS juddered, but the Land Rover didn't stop – it kept on going, skidding across the slippery mud.

What the hell was McKinnon screaming about? Couldn't see a bloody thing through all this filth.

Deep breath from the driver's seat. 'AAAAAAAAAAAAAA-AAAAAAAARGH!'

The Land Rover finally came to a halt and McKinnon sat there, teeth clenched, breath coming out in hard little puffs, like he was at antenatal class.

Roberta thumped him one. 'What the ferret-spudging hell is wrong with you?'

The windscreen wipers and rain finally managed to clear a couple of arcs through the muck...

Oh.

That lovely humpback bridge she'd tootled over in her MX-5 yesterday was gone. The only thing left was a stone pillar on the opposite bank of the *very* steep ravine. And between here and there: a granite-coloured rush of water battered past, tearing at the banks, its surface flecked with angry white spray as it wheeched a couple of full-sized trees past like they were paper boats.

And the Land Rover had slithered to a halt about six inches from where the road came to a sudden stop.

She took her feet off the dashboard and stared. 'Wow.'

McKinnon's breathing slowed to a hissing rasp. 'Don't move. *Please* don't move.'

He put the car in reverse and eased them back a good ten feet, before hauling on the handbrake and half-climbing/half-falling out into the pouring rain to stand there, gawping at the chasm they'd nearly skidded into. 'Ooh… Oh dear hairy…' He folded in half, grabbed his knees, and hyperventilated for a bit.

Had to admit, he kinda had a point.

But when you were kidding on you were a detective chief inspector, there were certain standards to maintain. So, Roberta dug into her jacket pocket and pulled out her mobile phone. Checked the display: no bars.

Typical. Couldn't be that easy, could it? Noooo…

She tucked the phone away and dug out her e-cigarette instead. About the size of a house-brick with a mouthpiece sticking out of one side. Flicked the switch and took a good long sook, holding the cherry-flavoured fog inside for a count of three before letting it loose in a Land-Rover-filling whoosh of steam. Humming Bach's 'Air on a G String' for good measure. 'Dum, da-dum, da, dum da-dum, da…'

McKinnon was still bent double, rain bouncing off the back of his stabproof vest. 'We could've died.'

Another whoosh of cherry. 'Dum, da-da-da-da-da-da-da, da-dada-da, da daaaa…'

'We nearly died, we nearly died, we nearly died…'

She leaned across the car and waved at him through the open driver's door. 'Hoy, Soggypants – there another way off this estate?'

He turned and said something, but it was drowned out by a snarling *roar* of thunder.

'What?'

McKinnon staggered and slipped his way back to the car, raising his voice over the rushing river and thumping rain.

'The only other way is up the Hangman's Ladder, over The Devil's Razor, then Deadfall Pass through the mountains.'

Why did country bumpkins always have to 'sexy' up their backwater locations with melodramatic place names? They weren't fooling anyone.

'Right, we'll try that, then.'

'Are you *insane*? In this weather, it'd be suicide!' He jabbed a hand at the missing bridge. 'WE NEARLY DIED!'

'You Highland bunnets are a bit … sensitive, aren't you?'

He hauled his soggy backside into the driver's seat and sat there dripping. 'Two climbers tried it last spring, and that was in the *sunshine*. Didn't find their bodies till autumn.' He started the engine and eased the Land Rover through a slow, oh-so-careful, three-point turn. Wincing every time they moved so much as an inch towards the ruined riverbank. 'We're going back to the castle.'

'Moan, whinge, gripe, complain.' Roberta let loose another fog of vape. 'In my day, lowly police constables did what they were told.'

Muscles clenched along the side of his jaw, but he kept his gob shut and didn't rise to it. Maybe the boy wasn't as thick as he looked? Good for him.

She clicked off her e-cigarette and put it away as the forest swallowed the car again. 'So, we're right back where we started from. No phone, no backup, and fifty-one people to interview.'

'Forty-*six* people.' Trying to sound all in control again, like she didn't know he'd probably crapped himself when they'd nearly gone over the edge.

'Oh aye? Let's hear it then, Sherlock.'

'I didn't kill him, Sergeant Moore didn't kill him.' McKinnon risked a quick glance across the car at her. 'I'm assuming *you* didn't kill him, and neither did your wife or my Barbara. That makes it forty-six left to interview.'

True.

Roberta stuck her feet back on the dashboard. 'What, no *Mrs* Sergeant Moore?'

'Not any more. And we don't talk about it if we know what's good for us.' The Land Rover splooshed through that huge puddle again, sending another wall of filthy water up over the bonnet and windscreen. McKinnon slowed them to a crawl, even though Certain Death at the Skirivour Rapids was in the opposite direction. 'His wife was having an affair with the local butcher, amongst others.'

Roberta sighed. 'I know you can judge a good butcher by the quality of their sausage, but you're no' meant to take that figuratively.'

'Lives in Australia now, with her "partner".' McKinnon made one-handed air quotes. 'Douglas, the bridegroom? Can't stand her. Said he'd rather drive burning nails into his balls than invite, and I quote, "that two-faced duplicitous bitch" to his wedding. His own mum!'

'Got to love a happy family.'

'So, now the Sarge just sits at home, on his own, watching movies, reading books, and painting landscapes.'

'Any good?'

PC McKinnon pulled a frog face and shook his head.

So much for Sergeant Moore the renaissance man.

The Land Rover turned onto a straight bit and the whole world lit up bright white as a massive slash of lightning ground-zeroed just ahead. The thunderclap slammed into the car before she could breathe, rattling the air in her lungs.

McKinnon slammed on the brakes again, the ABS's tremble joined by the screeching crackle of punished wood as a huge oak tree timbered down onto the road in front of them, leaving its scarred white stump behind.

Hitting the road in slow motion, the bounce of its leaves

and branches pounded in time with the blood in Roberta's ears.

The Land Rover slid to a halt a good thirty feet from the smouldering trunk.

They sat there, looking at it for a bit.

That was *twice* Mother Nature had tried to kill her today. Three times, if you counted the Hangover From Hell. Starting to feel a little personal, to be honest.

Roberta thumped McKinnon on the arm. 'Don't just sit there: get it shifted.'

He looked at her as if she'd just crapped on the dashboard. 'Shift it with *what*?'

'You've got a tow thing on the car. Use that.'

His mouth hung open for a moment, clearly absorbing her genius. 'It's a *massive* oak tree! It'll weigh at least fifteen, twenty tons – no way the Landy will pull it.'

Boy was an idiot.

'So, chop it into smaller bits!'

'What with, your cutting wit?' He made a show of patting down his stabproof vest. 'Because I seem to have left my chainsaw in my other suit.'

The only sound was the rain, clattering down on the Land Rover's roof.

Roberta narrowed her eyes. 'You're getting very cheeky for someone at risk of a punch in the nadgers from a superior officer.'

'Sorry, ma'am.' The tips of his ears went bright red.

Should think so too.

She pointed off into the woods. 'There a way around it?'

'Erm…?' A pained smile.

Wonderful. Just. Sodding. Wonderful.

Gah...

Didn't feel this long on the way out.

Rain hurtled down from the bruised sky, bouncing off the ground at her feet and drumming away on her pilfered umbrella, as Roberta slogged her way back along the road. Which, now that she had to walk along the bloody thing, turned out to be little more than a crappy track, full of rough bits, stones, and *bastarding* puddles.

Might as well stand in a bucket of lukewarm water, for all the protection her stupid shoes were giving.

And the high-vis raincoat McKinnon had dug out the back of the Land Rover stank of wet sheep. And the wetter it got, the more it stank. AND IT STANK A LOT.

McKinnon slumped along beside her, in a high-vis of his own, but where hers reached down past her knees, his was a proper size. Which meant everything from the waist down was getting drenched. Rain sparked off his peaked cap, great thick drips of it trickling down his neck and into his collar, where it was probably soaking him right through.

Good. Served the bugger right.

Yes, technically, she could be nice and let him share her brolly, but he was all: oh no, I couldn't *possibly*, it's a death trap waiting to happen in a lightning storm. Whinge, moan, complain.

Idiot.

You were more likely to win the lottery than get struck by lightning... Or was that the other way around? Roberta peered around the edge of her dripping umbrella at the lowering sky. Then ducked back in again.

Sod it, she'd take her chances.

And, if *that* wasn't bad enough, Sergeant Moore had been right about the temperature. Just gone eight and already the heat was beginning to build. The rain should've cooled everything down, but it just made the air muggy and humid. And having to wear a thick, padded, high-vis horror waterproof wasn't helping either.

A thin trickle of sweat waltzed its way down her spine and into her pants, more prickling out beneath Old Faithful's underband.

Ugh...

She gave McKinnon the gift of a good hard glower. 'This is all *your* fault.'

'But I didn't—'

'I don't know *how* it's your fault yet, but I'll work it out. And see when I do...?'

His face fell as that sank in. Bet he wished they'd gone over the edge and into the river, now. Really wasn't his lucky day, was it?

They lumbered on through the rain.

Mud. Mud all the way up past her knees. About half of it was from sploshing their way along the stupid waterlogged track, the other half following an unfortunate incident involving a particularly slippy bit and landing on her arse.

At least McKinnon had the good sense not to laugh. Otherwise he'd be wearing that bloody peaked cap of his as a suppository. He cleared his throat. 'So ... have you worked out who did it? Who killed Sir Reginald?'

'Give us a chance, haven't even interviewed anyone yet!'

'Only I thought, with the deductive thing you did at the bar? You know, when we first met?'

Roberta stopped in the middle of the track and turned to give his arm a good hard punch.

'Ow!'

'You didn't actually believe all that Sherlock Holmes nonsense, did you? You arrived at the hotel in your uniform, you laminated wanknumpty! I *saw* you.'

He stood there, staring at her, wearing the kind of expression a small child does when you tell them Santa Claus doesn't actually exist and their gerbil isn't off living on a lovely farm, it's dead and flushed down the toilet.

She hit him again.

'Ow!'

'Come on.' Roberta squelched off, but he stayed where he was. And when she looked over her shoulder, he was still there, staring after her, sort of hunched in on himself.

Oh, for God's sake...

Her shoulders slumped. Then she turned and stomped back through the mud, till she was standing in front of him again. 'All right, all right – I'm sorry I called you a wanknumpty. OK?'

His face doubled down on the spanked-puppy look. 'We're not going to catch the killer, are we.' Said as a statement, not a question.

Might as well throw him a bone, I suppose.

She forced a cheery tone into her voice. 'Of *course* we are, because we're the good guys!' This time the punch on his arm was a lot more gentle and playful. 'See?'

He deflated even further. 'We're going to bumble along, messing things up, till the real police get here from Inverness and take over.'

Roberta took hold of his shoulder with her free hand and gave him a squeeze. Spelling it out, nice and slow: 'We – will – catch – the – killer.'

He looked down at his feet and nodded, *clearly* not believing her. But at least this time when she scuffed off he slouched along beside her. Sighing with every third step. Like the massive pain in the jacksie he was.

She stepped around a puddle. 'This dodgy goldmine, was it just the locals got burned, or was it Sir Whatsisname's mates too?'

'Probably.' Voice flat and miserable. 'Well, maybe some of them. You don't screw over your *real* friends, do you?'

'True.'

But that was typical of the landed gentry, wasn't it? Why rip-off your posh mates when you could stick it to the working class instead? Make the peasants pay for your champagne-and-caviar lifestyle while *they* struggle along on Buckfast-and-sliced-white.

The path turned left up ahead and – hold on to your sweat-soggied arse-munchingly uncomfortable Brazilian pants – that pair of stone pillars with the wrought iron, 'SKIRIVOUR CASTLE HOTEL' above it hove into view.

About bloody time.

Twenty feet past that and it was the castle's turn, lurking there in all its rain-lashed ugliness.

Roberta squelched towards the gloomy pile, frowning as something stirred in the depths of her brain. Something... 'You ever read *Murder on the Orient Express*?'

McKinnon shrugged. 'Nah, I don't really do books. The Sarge is your man for that kind of thing, loves his crime novels.'

'Pin back your lugs and learn something, then.' She stopped, looking up at their very own blot on the landscape. 'In *Murder on the Orient Express*, this slimy American gets bumped off and Hercule Poirot has to figure out who did it. Only it wasn't just *one* murderer, they *all* killed him – everyone on the train.'

'Aye...' PC McKinnon pulled a face. 'Seems a bit far-fetched. I mean, it's hard enough getting four people to agree on where to go for dinner, can you imagine getting a whole train-load to do it about murdering someone?'

Philistine. 'It's a *classic* of modern literature.'

'You'd be there all year!' He counted the points off on his fingers. 'To get anything done you'd need to elect a chairman, which means setting up a voting system, then there's regular meetings, somewhere to meet, agendas—'

'All right, nobody likes a smartarse.'

He started on the other hand. '—someone to take minutes, probably a bunch of subcommittees about stuff like alibis and killing methods—'

She thumped the back of her hand against his chest. 'I'm no' saying the *whole town* murdered Sir Buggerlugs, it's—'

'And even if it *was* logistically possible, where would everyone in the village hide? They weren't invited to the wedding and they can't have sneaked off in this weather with the bridge out. They'd be every bit as stuck as we are!'

She gave him another thump. 'I liked you better when you were cringing in awe-struck reverence.'

'You did ask.'

'Hmph...' Roberta marched off, past the dribbly fountain and under the big portico with its miserable bunting. Clicked her umbrella shut and gave it a good shake, sending water flying like a soggy terrier.

'I'm sure it's a good book, it's just a very silly idea.'

She shoved through the double doors into the hotel lobby again. Jammed the umbrella back in the thing. Peeled off her high-vis raincoat and thrust it into the cultureless idiot's arms. 'You've no' got a clue about proper literature.'

Sergeant Moore appeared from the other side of that huge metal stag. Face all creased and worried. 'Where did you pair disappear off to?'

McKinnon unbuttoned his raincoat. 'Bridge is out. Must've got washed away in the night.'

'Aye, and there's sod-all mobile signal out there either.' She squished and squelched past the pair of them, making for the stairs.

'I could've told you that.' Sergeant Moore fell into step beside her, holding out a couple sheets of paper. 'I've made a list of everyone and ranked it in order of who hated him the most to least.'

'Aye, I got the low-down from your wee loon, there; every bugger for a hundred miles hated our victim.' The steps creaked beneath her saturated shoes. 'Don't blame them either: man was a dick.'

Sergeant Moore stopped at the bottom of the stairs, frowning up at her. 'Where are you off to *now*?'

Roberta kept on going. 'Getting changed. Everything from the waist down's dripping. And no' in a sexy way!'

And believe it or not, the rude sod had the cheek to shudder at the thought.

9

Susan sat in that high-backed armchair by the window, scowling at the rain. Disapproval oozing out of her like stink from a chunk of forgotten haggis, festering away at the back of the fridge. Honestly, the woman could hold a grudge better than anyone.

Ah well, nothing Roberta could do about it now, standing there naked from the waist down, towelling her lower half – working a bit of life back into the cold, pale, wobbly skin. And that wasn't cellulite, thank you very much, it was goose pimples. Because it was much colder *inside* this old pile than out.

Her stripy pair of soggy socks sagged over the hotel room's radiator, but the jeans had to be abandoned in the bath, draped over the shower rail. Dripping.

Susan gave a pointed sniff as Roberta moved on to one set of wrinkled toes. 'I don't see why *I* have to be confined to my room like some sort of criminal.'

Again.

No point rising to it, she was spoiling for a fight – could see that a mile off. She had her spoiling-for-a-fight face on. Mouth pinched. Chin up. Arms folded, squishing her boobs down as she pressed herself back into the chair.

'Can we no' do this right now?'

Susan's eyes got harder. 'Bad enough you humiliated me last night without—'

'A man's been murdered, OK? And yes, he was a *shitty* man who screwed everyone over, but he was still murdered and that means we all have to make sacrifices. All of us.' Roberta finished her drowned-corpse feet, dumped the towel on the bed, and had a rummage about inside her suitcase. Had to be another pair of pants in here somewhere...

'You just want me out of the way.'

'Oh, for God's sake.' Muttering it *just* loud enough to make sure it was audible. Roberta stood, a pair of big grey pants clutched in one hand – the elastic gone a bit hairy around the waistband. 'Look, I've got to go catch a killer, so can we—'

'And those!' Susan released an arm to point at the pants. 'I bought you three nice new sets of decent underwear – they were *La Perla*, have you any idea how expensive they were? Did you even try them on?'

A sigh. 'I had the black lacy ones on yesterday and spent the whole time hauling half of it out the crack of my—'

'And what about the bra?' Teeth bared, working herself up. 'Because you weren't wearing it at the wedding, were you? No, you were wearing that horrible ancient grey thing!'

'It made my boobs all—'

'Is that why we don't have sex any more? You don't even *try*, Robbie. I'm just some sort of shapeless sexless blob to you!'

Roberta just stared at her.

It was only underwear, for Christ's sake. Underwear apparently designed for flat-chested stick insects who didn't mind six inches of lacy netting jammed up their bumhole. Why the hell did it—

Susan's voice turned brittle and sharp. 'You're having an affair, aren't you.'

What?

'No!'

She grabbed a tartan cushion from the armchair and hurled

it at Roberta. 'That's why you won't wear nice things for *me*, you're too busy wearing them for someone else!'

Roberta hauled on her huge grey pants with the hairy elastic. 'I'm no' having an affair! How could I? Look at me!'

'So, what, you just don't find me sexy any more?'

The woman was insane. Certifiably, clinically, insane.

'Sexy? Find you *sexy*? Susan, the sun rises *in you*. The moon sets *in you*. The oceans rise and fall because of *you*. You're everything!' The room got a bit swimmy at that – don't you dare cry! – and Roberta's throat tightened, making her voice creak. 'It's...' Sagging a bit. 'It's *me* I don't find sexy.' She pulled her T-shirt up, showing off those ugly pants and her ugly stomach with its rash of midge bites. Took a double handful of pale flabby belly and squeezed it. Like lardy Play-doh. 'I'm fat and I'm old and I'm horrible.' She let go of the horrorbelly and wiped the tears from her cheeks with her palms. 'OK?'

Susan stood, nodded, then swept her up into a hug, squeezing the breath out of her, holding her. 'Then let's grow old and fat and sexy together.' She reached down and gave Roberta's bum a grope, voice a dirty whisper: 'No time like the present.'

Sir Reginald Bradbury-Scott's body dangled above them, willy out.

Roberta grinned at Sergeant Moore and PC McKinnon, fingers wrapped around a mug of hotel-room-packet-hot-chocolate. All warm and sweet and melty inside. Just like her. She'd changed into her last dry pair of jeans, second-last dry pair of socks, and the Converse trainers she'd turned up in yesterday. Sort of an investigative-casual outfit for the pretend detective chief inspector about town.

McKinnon and Moore watched her from a safe distance, as if she was about to do something horrible to them. Possibly with a six-foot fencepost.

It was Sergeant Moore who plucked up the courage first. 'OK, I'll bite: what?'

She cranked the grin up a bit. 'Nothing.'

McKinnon backed off a pace. He'd changed out of his soggy police-issue itchy trousers and black boots, and into a pair of old jeans and grey Crocs. They didn't really go with the stabproof vest, high-vis and peaked cap. 'Aye, but you're positively *glowing*.'

'Just love being a police officer.' A sip of scalding hot brown. To be honest, it smelled a lot better than it tasted, but Susan made it and it was the thought that counted. 'Right: so the bridge is out, all communication's down, we've got a killer on the loose, and fifty-one suspects. I miss anything?'

'Forty-six, remember?'

The wee loon was right. Fifty-one, less the three of them and their respective bonk buddies. All except for poor old *unshaggable* Sergeant Moore…

She tilted her head on one side and frowned at him, standing there in his country-club polo shirt and chinos. No wonder his willy was surplus to requirements. Got to put a bit of effort in if you wanted sexytimes. 'What happened to Mrs Moore, then?'

His cheeks flushed. 'We're divorced.'

'I know that, you daft spud. I mean: how come she's not here to see her son getting married? Thought that was every mother's dream?'

The blush darkened. 'Anyway, won't be long till it's hoaching with flies in here. Already getting hotter.'

McKinnon rolled his eyes. 'The crime-scene manual clearly states—'

'And you remember how long it took them to rebuild the bridge after last time? Never mind days, we could be here for weeks.'

'Yes, but—'

'Be nothing left of the body by then, just a pile of bones on the floor.'

Roberta hardened her frown into a scowl. 'You pair are seriously harshing my mellow here.'

He spread his hands. 'All I'm saying is: *circumstances change*, and if we don't do something there's going to be no crime scene left to preserve. The bugs will have eaten it all.' He curled his lip. 'And can you imagine the *smell*? Even if the forecast's wrong and it only hits twenty degrees, the whole hotel's going to stink like a charnel pit.'

Well *that* was romantic.

How were you supposed to enjoy a good romp with your wife when the stink of rotting corpse was slithering in under the bedroom door? That'd dampen your ardour.

She looked up at their dead knight and his shrivelled willy. 'Mind you, how can I catch a murderer if we've no clue how or where our victim actually died?'

Moore nodded. 'Exactly! At least if the Scene Examiners and the Pathologist were here, we'd have something to go on. But with the bridge out…?'

'Ooh, ooh!' McKinnon did his bouncing up and down thing. 'We've got stuff for taking fingerprints in the crime-scene kit, if that helps?'

He was kinda sweet, in his own way, but clearly thick as mince.

'Oh aye, that'll be a *great* help.' Roberta gave him her best innocent smile. The one that every PC in NE Division had learned to fear. 'And what, pray tell, are we going to do with any fingerprints you find? Will we be able to run them through the system with no phone lines? No internet connection? Mobile signal?'

His face fell a bit at that. 'Ah.'

'*Maybe* we can leave them at the bottom of the garden, and the Fingerprint Fairies will spirit them off to Magic Pixie La-La-Land, so the Great Goblin can sprinkle unicorn powder on them and tell us which of the guests they match?'

'Well, it—'

'Or are you planning on doing it yourself, by hand? Trained in fingerprint analysis, are we? Got our own magnifying glass and deerstalker?' She thumped him. 'Didn't think so.'

He stared at his boots. 'Sorry, ma'am.'

'Go see if you can find us a couple of long ladders. And make sure you wear gloves! Killer might have been at one of them.'

McKinnon scurried off.

Sergeant Moore watched him go. 'He was only trying to help.'

'You go find the laundry. I want a couple of double sheets, clean as you can get them.'

'I know he's young, but Mikey's not as daft as he looks. He's a good kid.'

'He's an idiot.' She pointed off into the hotel. 'Go. Sheets.'

Sergeant Moore sighed, then turned and wandered off, shaking his head.

Leaving Roberta on her own with the body.

A middle-aged man, crucified on a big metal stag's antlers, with his pyjama bottoms round his ankles. Moore was right, it wasn't really dignified, was it? Even if Sir Reginald Bradbury-Scott *was* a dick.

She nodded at his corpse. 'Right, listen up: I didn't like you, and you didn't like me. And I think we can both now agree that you were wrong and I was right about that. But I *will* do my best to find out who killed you. Even if they had good reason and you deserved it.' Quick swig of mediocre hot chocolate. 'Fair enough?'

Sir Reginald just dangled there.

But then some people were just rude that way.

'There we go.' PC McKinnon stood back, hands on his hips, admiring his handiwork. Like he'd just painted the roof of the Sistine Chapel, single-handed, instead of stuck up a couple of large A-frame ladders in a hotel lobby.

On the plus side, they were easily big enough to reach the body.

Sergeant Moore rubbed his hands. 'This'll be one in the eye for Inverness. Our solving the case before they even hear about it? Serve the credit-stealing bunch of bastards right.'

'We've no' solved anything yet.' Roberta gave McKinnon a poke. 'Hold the ladder for us, there's a good lad.'

He ducked in under the A-frame and took a good firm grip of the legs, watching as she clang-clanged her way to the top.

Up close, Sir Reginald Bradbury-Scott was *not* having a good day.

Six inches of metal antlers poked through his chest, just below nipple height, one on either side. Little more than a crusting of dried red around the puncture wounds, so he was *definitely* already dead by the time they'd skewered him up here. One horn through the palm of his left hand, one horn through the wrist of his right. His eyes were open, mouth too, head tilted back to stare at the ceiling. Wearing an expression of slightly startled melancholy – like the stuffed stags' heads on the wall.

Only, unlike the taxidermied animals, he didn't have a hard plastic tongue.

He had *something,* though.

Was that…?

She leaned in closer, peering into his gob.

There *was* something in there. Something made of fabric. Too dark to see properly.

She took out her phone and turned on the torch app, but it didn't make any difference. Whatever it was, it was black and a little bit shiny. No idea what, though.

Hmm…

While she had her phone out, she set it to record, filming all the bits the pathologist would complain about most when they finally got here. Puncture wounds, points of contact, face, hands, little shrivelled willy. They'd still whinge about lack of proper procedure, but what choice did she have? It was either this or let the maggots have him.

Roberta put her phone away and clanged down the ladder again. 'Right, up you go the pair of you: let's get him down.'

PC McKinnon's face soured as he looked up at the remains. 'Could you not have pulled his pyjama bottoms back up?'

'Don't be so homophobic, you're not going to catch anything off a dead man's willy. Now: gloves on and up!'

A slump, a groan, then McKinnon snapped on a pair of blue nitriles and climbed.

Sergeant Moore pulled on a set of gloves too. Nodded at the other A-frame. 'Going to hold the ladder?'

'Supervising, aren't I? So *try* to no' fall off, eh? One dead body's enough of a pain without you joining in.'

While the pair of them scaled their respective rungs, she grabbed the folded sheets and unfurled them on the tartan carpet beneath the ladders. That should do it.

The first thing PC McKinnon did when he got level with the body, was pull its PJ bottoms up, keeping his head as far away from Sir Reginald's cold dead naked crotch as possible.

Child.

Sergeant Moore made it to the top of his ladder, and the two of them set about pulling Sir Reginald off the antlers. The left hand and right wrist came away fairly easily, but the torso needed a lot more grunting and swearing. Then a sort of Velcro scratchy *screltching* noise as they wrestled him up and off the metal spikes that stuck through his chest.

It set both sets of ladders wobbling so hard she had to stop supervising and run forward to stabilise the damn things. 'Don't drop him!'

God, the pathologist would *love* that.

More grunting and swearing as they manhandled him over Sergeant Moore's shoulder, after which it was a pretty straightforward fireman's carry down to the ground.

Roberta slapped McKinnon on the back, hard enough to set him staggering. 'See? What were you moaning about: piece of cake.'

Sergeant Moore lowered the body onto the sheets and stood back, rubbing at the small of his back. 'Should we say something?'

'Aye: wrap him up.'

The two of them did, folding the sheets around Sir Reginald and tucking in the ends – until he looked like a very large chrysalis. Or a really badly rolled joint.

She pointed at Moore. 'You: take the shoulders.' Then at McKinnon. 'You: take his feet. I'll get the doors.'

Took a bit, but they eventually got him lifted, the body sagging in the middle like a half-bent paperclip that rocked from side to side as Roberta led the way across the lobby.

Sergeant Moore shifted his grip on the slithery sheets. 'Where are we going?'

'Where do you think?'

10

Roberta dumped the last net of carrots onto the stack just outside the walk-in fridge's door, meaning the big wire shelf they'd occupied was now empty.

PC McKinnon and Sergeant Moore lowered Sir Reginald's body onto the cleared space, their breaths misting in the cold air. You'd never think McKinnon was the youngest of them, his face all flushed and sweaty from carrying the body down here, steam rising from his arms and shoulders as he puffed and panted. Moore wasn't even breathing hard.

'Pfff...' McKinnon pulled his hat off and wiped a hand across his soggy forehead. 'Doesn't ... seem ... very dignified.'

Sergeant Moore shrugged. 'Compared to hanging in reception with his willy out? I'd say it's definitely an improvement.'

'True.' McKinnon bent double and grabbed his own knees. 'Argh... Talk about ... a dead weight!'

Roberta wiped her carroty hands on a box of mushrooms. 'Have you two finished?'

'See?' A tut from Moore. 'That's the trouble with you new lot, back in my day: you joined the job, you played rugby and shinty against the other police forces. Climbed mountains in your spare time.'

McKinnon brought his shiny face up. 'I'm in ... the chess club.'

'Chess isn't a *sport*, Mikey, it's a cry for help from people who can't get laid.'

'Hey!'

'Enough.' Roberta pointed. 'I want a padlock on that fridge door, and to hell with anyone who complains they can't have bacon with their full Scottish…' Wait a minute. 'Well, maybe no' the bacon. Or sausages. Or black pudding.' She checked her watch again: just gone ten, and no breakfast yet. A rumbling growl sounded deep within her belly, because a DIY sandwich of pilfered leftovers, four hours ago, didn't count. 'Anyone else starving?'

PC McKinnon and Sergeant Moore looked at each other.

Too polite to say anything. Must be.

She gave the wee loon a poke. 'When it's breakfast time … well, suppose we'd better call it brunchtime, now – you'll just have to stand guard. Make sure no one gets served a portion of gammon with their eggs.' They'd need to plan it, though. Couldn't have the guests running loose in the hotel; who knew what they'd get up to? Have to keep the buggers segregated till they'd all been interviewed. 'Bring them down in small batches, they're no' allowed to talk to each other, and after brunch everyone goes right back to their rooms. No exceptions. Then you patrol the hotel: stop the buggers sneaking out to shag a neighbour or plant evidence.'

Sergeant Moore pulled a face. 'But—'

'You're the one said they'd all need fed and watered, remember? Besides, the Procurator Fiscal's going to string us up for moving the body anyway, might as well get a decent nosh-up out of it.'

The sound of clattering pots and frying pans echoed through from the kitchen, reverberating around the walk-in fridge, bringing with it the dark mysterious scent of sizzling bacon and other delicious things. Not-so-muffled voices, as orders were shouted and fulfilled.

'*Need two full Scottish with scrambled, and a poached egg on haddock! Brown toast!*'

Clang bash. Then a harsh French accent: '*Stovies 'ash, beetroot compote, deux œufs sur le plat, for table six. Service!*'

All right for some, getting their faces fed while other poor sods had to keep working.

Bet PC McKinnon was nibbling away on a bacon buttie when he was meant to be standing guard too. He looked the type.

Roberta unwrapped the last corner of sheet from Sir Reginald's head, the fabric squeaky in her blue-nitrile-gloved fingers.

Sergeant Moore looked down at the dead face and shuddered. 'Are you sure about this? I mean, moving the body to a secure location's one thing, but—'

'It's a clue. Can't catch Buffalo Bill without clues, Clarice.' She made the Hannibal Lecter 'nice glass of chianti' sound, but Moore just stared at her.

'Nah, you've lost me there.'

'*Silence of the Lambs?*'

That got her a puzzled shrug.

Seriously?

Thought he was meant to be into movies?

'Oh, come on, you *must've* seen *Silence of the Lambs*! The victim's got a death's-head moth in his throat? That's how we know the killer's into metamorphosis?'

'Sorry.'

Unbelievable. 'I'm working with cultural philistines.' She

puffed out a deep, disappointed breath, then went back to the body. Cupping the jaw between her hands and wobbling the whole head from side to side. Moved without a problem – nice and loose. 'No sign of rigor mortis, so death was probably between twelve and eighteen hours ago. Six hours to get stiff, six hours being stiff, six hours to go floppy again. Like with Viagra.' She gave Moore a wink and he blushed. 'Attend enough post mortems and something's bound to rub off.' Like morbid frottage.

'It's...' he checked his watch, 'twenty-five to ten. Eighteen hours ago we'd only just finished the ceremony. They were still doing photographs.'

'Well, maybe he's at the *getting*-stiff stage, then? Time of death's more an art than a science. That's why pathologists make such a production out of it.'

She worked her fingers down and in, feeling her way through that suspiciously dark mop of hair, which was *definitely* dyed, because a teeny sliver of grey roots was just visible where they joined the scalp.

Ooh, now that was interesting.

The fingers on her right hand explored the indentation again. Little hard bits moving beneath the skin, about the diameter of a golf ball. Like someone had been a bit too rough with a chocolate Easter egg.

'Got a squishy bit at the back here, on the right – well, my right, not his – the skull's gone crackly.'

'Blunt instrument to the back of the head?'

'Probably.' She let go and held her hand up, rubbing her fingertips together in the fridge's cold light. A tiny smear of dark red marked the blue nitrile. 'Or he fell on something. Difficult to say without X-rays.' Frown. 'Anyway, time for the main event.' She tilted Sir Reginald's head back and opened his mouth wide. Took her phone and shone its torch inside.

'Well? Is it a moth?'

'Course it's no' a moth.' Black and a little bit shiny. Fabric. All balled up in there. She held out her hand. 'Pass us those tongs.'

He did.

To be honest, they were far too large, clearly the kind of implements more suited to burning sausages on a barbecue than performing delicate post-mortem procedures, the tips covered in thick red silicone. Still, it wasn't like Sir Reginald was going to complain, was it?

Roberta went fishing in his gaping mouth, pinching an edge of fabric between the silicone points. 'Gotcha!' She pulled whatever it was free and held it aloft in triumph. Where it promptly unfurled itself like a little black flag, revealing its true nature. 'Oh.'

Sergeant Moore cleared his throat. 'Dearie me...'

The 'thing' stuffed down Sir Reginald Bradbury-Scott's throat was a pair of lacy silk panties. Expensive ones, not end-of-season-bargain-bin Ann Summers. A thong, though, so even more bumcrackular than the Brazilian ones Susan had bought. 'Well, I guess that explains why his PJs were round his ankles.'

'Dirty old bugger.' The smile faded on Moore's face. 'You don't think we should check he's not been ... you know, erm ... *interfered* with. Sexually.'

Roberta raised an eyebrow. 'You any idea how to do that?'

A grimace and a shaken head.

'Didn't think so.' She lowered the panties into a pilfered freezer bag and tied the top. Didn't look as if they'd been worn – no handy stains on the gusset – but maybe, when the cavalry arrived, they could get some DNA off the things? 'So, we've narrowed it down to: sexual adventure goes horribly wrong; jilted lover takes revenge; or jealous husband, in the library, with a claw-hammer.'

Sergeant Moore snapped off his nitrile gloves. 'Or business deal turns sour and the killer makes it look like something kinky to hide their tracks.'

True.

She frowned at the partially cocooned body. Lot of possible motives there, which didn't exactly help whittle down their list of suspects. Only one way to make any progress, then.

Roberta wrapped the sheets over Sir Reginald Bradbury-Scott's face again. 'Get breakfast down you, then we start interrogating folk. See if we can't find ourselves a murderer.'

Sergeant Moore stifled a belch. 'Sorry. Shouldn't have eaten that second hash-brown-and-black-pudding-buttie.' Greedy sod.

Roberta sooked the last remnants of sticky savoury sweetness from her fingers and pointed at the door in front of them. The one marked 'B UNNAHABHAIN'. 'Ready when you are.'

The hotel was strangely silent with everyone confined to their rooms. Well, except for whoever was taking their turn eating a silent breakfast in the dining room under the watchful eye of PC McKinnon. Assuming he hadn't snuck off for fourths, that is.

Moore hesitated, his knuckles six inches from the wood. 'Can I just bring up the value of interviewing them separately again? Only—'

'No, unless you want my boot up your bum.' Wiping her sooked fingers dry on her jeans. 'Anyway, each couple's been cooped up together since about six this morning. A fiver gets you twenty they've spent the whole time rehearsing their stories.' She thumped his arm with the back of her hand. 'Now: arse in gear.'

Moore checked his notebook and knocked – none of that namby-pamby stuff this time, proper hard police-officer belts. 'Mr Reeves? It's the police, can you open up, please?'

Roberta settled back against the wall, a wee smile frolicking across her face. Had to admit, life seemed a lot better after a wriggle with the wife and a stack of sticky maple bacon pancakes. Should definitely do that more often.

Still nothing from 'BUNNAHABHAIN'.

She was about to tell Sergeant Moore to give the door another hammering when it creaked open and a fusty bloke in his late sixties opened it and scowled out at them. Probably going for outraged-but-upstanding-member-of-the-community, but it was a difficult look to carry off when you resembled a half-sooked lollypop that'd been trapped down the back of the sofa for a couple of weeks.

He stuck his nose in the air. Accent so posh you'd need a silver fish knife to cut it. 'Are we to be permitted to leave our room, or is this a police state now?'

'Mr Reeves.' Sergeant Moore gave him a bland smile. 'We'll only take a couple minutes of your time, sir.'

A big, I'm-so-important, sigh, and he led them into a bedroom that was almost identical to Roberta and Susan's. Only tartanier.

A woman sat in a straight-backed wooden chair by the little desk. Luckily, she was every bit as warm and welcoming as her husband had been. As if someone had stuffed sixteen stone of cold malevolence into a fourteen-stone bag.

Roberta settled herself on the end of the bed, bouncing a couple of times to test the springs. 'On you go, Sergeant.'

He flipped his notebook open and stood there with pen poised. 'Mr Reeves, I understand you and Sir Reginald weren't on the best of terms?'

Mr Reeves gave Roberta the kind of look probably reserved for the revolting lower classes. 'Sir Reginald and I were *very* good friends, we played golf together. We may have had our differences in the past, but that's all water under the bridge, now. He was a decent chap. The kind of chap that any chap would be jolly lucky to count as a friend.' Chest out. 'Won't hear a bad word said about the man!'

Mrs Reeves nodded. 'Quite right, Hugo.'

'Salt of the earth.'

'I'll bet he was.' Roberta stopped bouncing. 'So, what was this falling out about?'

'A mere misunderstanding. All forgiven and forgotten, *as I said.*'

'Aye, right...' She raised an eyebrow. 'And, now he's dead, you're going to pretend everything was hunky-dory?'

A smug, smarmy smile pulled that sooked-lollypop face out of shape. 'If it wasn't, I'd hardly be attending his daughter's wedding, now would I?'

Condescending prick.

'LAGAVULIN' was just as tartany as 'BUNNAHABHAIN'. Roberta lounged by the window, leaning against the wall as Sergeant Moore took down the long and boring anecdote Mortimer Beresford *still* hadn't finished telling.

'And I know corporate law can be a bit cut-throat at times, but as I always say to your good lady wife, "Susan," I say, "Susan, it could be worse, at least we're not merchant bankers!"' He'd ditched last night's morning suit in favour of a pair of corduroy trousers in an apoplectic shade of burgundy and a pink shirt. Still had on far too much jewellery, though. He gave her an apologetic smile. 'Sorry we can't be more help.'

His wife – what was it, Agatha? Agnes? Abigail? – placed a hand on his shoulder. For some reason, she'd thought it was a good idea to dress in the same clothes as her husband. Like some bizarre before-and-after photograph. 'And don't forget all that money Sir Reginald raised for Romanian orphans, Mortimer.'

His whole face seemed to blossom at that. 'Oh yes, quite right! Upright chap, Reggie. A real character.'

The only thing to differentiate 'GLENDRONACH' from every other bedroom they'd visited so far was the view. This one overlooked the waterlogged car park with its collection of drowning vehicles.

Mr and Mrs Ratchett had probably gone for 'business casual', but ended up looking like a pair of yuppies well past their sell-by date. They clearly hadn't got the memo that the Eighties were over. Or if they *had*, they'd left it in their Filofax.

Mrs Ratchett made a proper pantomime show of thinking about it, tapping her fingertips against her almost non-existent chin. 'I *think*, what I liked most about Sir Reginald was his … his *generosity* of spirit, didn't you, Adrian?'

A nod. 'Oh definitely. Generosity of spirit.'

'Always thinking of others, wasn't he?'

'Always. Always thinking of others.'

She clenched her hands to her bosom. 'It's just so terrible to think he's gone…'

'Terrible, just terrible. He was the salt of the earth.'

Now, 'CRAGGANMORE' was a bit grander than the bedrooms they'd been in so far. A junior suite, which meant you didn't get a sitting room, but you did get a putting machine and a bedroom big enough for a couch. The sideboard behind it played host to an ice bucket, full of fresh ice cubes, and a bottle of something fizzy and expensive. Which was odd, given that everyone *including* the hotel staff were meant to be on lockdown.

The room's occupant had the kind of head you could probably use to bang nails in, a short rectangular body and strangely tiny feet. No business casual for him, though, he was done up in an expensive-looking suit, with perfectly manicured nails, a porcelain-white smile featuring a gold tooth at the front, and a full-on Kremlin-issue accent. Smiling as he poured himself another glass of champagne. 'Meester Bradbury-Scott, he was good man. Very trustworthy.'

Sergeant Moore wrote that down. 'I hear you and he had a falling out over some investments in Edinburgh, Mr … Volkov?'

'Please, you call me Maksim.' He flashed that gold tooth again. 'This was … misunderstanding. He come to me and he say, "Maksim Arturovich, we must to be *friends* again, no more fighting. Is bad for business, yes?" So, we drink vodka and, how you say, bury the axe?'

Roberta peered out the window. His view was better too – across the trees to what looked like a wee stone circle, lurking in the downpour. 'Takes a lot for someone *like you* to forgive someone like Bradbury-Scott. Treating you with disrespect? *Conning* you?' She turned back to the room. 'Wouldn't like that.'

'Someone like me?' A modest shrug. 'I am simple flower merchant, I have no problem can not be made go away with good friendship.' He gave her a wink, toasting her with his champagne flute. 'And good *vodka!*' Knocking back the whole glass, then sighing and shaking his head. 'It is *great* shame about Meester Bradbury-Scott, he was, how you say…?'

'Salt of the earth?'

Maksim Arturovich Volkov's gold-toothed smile returned. 'Yes! This is it *exactly*. Salt of the earth.'

Of course it sodding was.

Sergeant Moore eased the door to 'CRAGGANMORE' closed, then stood there frowning at it while Roberta had a sly puff on her e-cigarette – filling the corridor with cherry-scented steam. Like a wee fruity dragon.

She had a bash at a smokeless smoke ring. It looked like a Moomin with piles. '"Flower merchant" my sharny arse. If he's a flower merchant, I'm a sack of geraniums.'

'You starting to see a pattern here?'

'No one's that universally beloved. No one.' Her second go at a smoke ring wasn't much better, more legless sheep than doughnut. 'You know what I think? I think...'

Hang on a minute.

Roberta hurried over to the window, squinting out the rain-pebbled glass. There was *someone out there*. A figure, barely visible through the downpour. 'There! You see that?'

'See what?'

She thumped a fingertip against the glass. 'There: disappearing into the trees?'

Couldn't make out much detail from this distance, but it was definitely a person, at the far end of the castle's manicured gardens, disappearing into the woods.

Moore stared. 'Everyone's supposed to be confined to their rooms.'

She stuffed her e-cigarette away and lurched into a run. 'Well don't just stand there!'

Along the corridor, skidding around the corner and down the sweeping wooden steps, taking them two at a time and across the lobby floor. Sprinting past the huge body-less stag. Wheeching the soggy high-vis raincoats off the coatstand by the door and thumping out into the dreich and drookit afternoon.

11

Roberta hurled one of the soggy high-vis jackets at Moore, struggling into her own as they hurtled around the side of the hotel, gravel crunching beneath their feet.

Then a hard left, running across the squelchy grass, rain crackling against her back and soaking into her hair as they made for the gap in the trees where the unknown sneaky bugger had vanished.

Roberta zipped herself up. 'You got your cuffs on you?'

'I'm in civvies!'

'How are we supposed to arrest them without cuffs?'

The grass got longer closer to the woods, snatching at their legs with long wet tendrils, then whooooomph, they were in beneath the canopy of pine and beech.

Gloom wrapped itself around them – what little sunlight there was, banished by the thick lid of leaves. That dark brown earthy smell of damp vegetation and waterlogged earth. A toilet-cleaner whiff of pine.

No sign of their mysterious figure, but a thin trail twisted off into the forest ahead.

Roberta lumbered down it, getting slower, each breath more of a struggle than the last. Sweating like a bastard in this rotten high-vis too. Puffing and panting. Till a dagger lanced in under her ribs, yanking her to a halt, one hand clutching her side. 'Arg… Stitch, stitch!'

Sergeant Moore pushed past. 'Get out the way!' And he was off, running full tilt along the path, disappearing into the woods.

She bent double, clutching her knees and wheezing like an elderly Jack Russell terrier.

Should really ... should really exercise more ... Join ... join a gym ... Eat fewer ... pies.

Pfff...

Getting old, Roberta.

Old and slow.

Finally, the ache in her side faded and she straightened up. Puffed out a few hot breaths and wiped the mix of rain and sweat from her face. Rummled her hands through her wet hair. Managed a sort of limping jog, following the path again.

It twisted and turned, around trees, bushes, more trees.

Probably not even a path. Probably a rabbit track. Completely unsuitable for fully grown women who were a bit less fit than they used to be. It vanished under fallen logs, only to reappear on the other side, jinked around swollen mounds of sickly mushrooms – their yellow domes glistening like unsqueezed plukes.

And then it disappeared completely.

Because why not make things *even worse* than they already were?

Roberta did a slow three-sixty, peering out into the dark woods.

No sign of anyone. The only sound: the patter of rain filtering through leaves to drip onto the loam below.

'Sergeant Moore?'

No reply.

She did another slow-motion pirouette.

Where the hell had the idiot got to?

She cupped her hands either side of her mouth and dragged in a deep breath. 'SERGEANT MOORE!'

There wasn't even an echo – the forest swallowed it whole.

Oh, *well done*, Roberta. Take the daft sod out into the woods and get him killed by some murderous maniac.

Another deep breath. 'SERGEANT MOORE!'

Still nothing. Just the dripping and the gloom and the eerie rows of bone-grey trees beneath that dark lid of branches and leaves.

'Come on, Roberta, think!'

Well, standing here wasn't helping, was it?

She picked a direction at random and pushed on, deeper into the woods. Past more fallen trees. He must've left a trail, right? Broken twigs and footprints and all that malarkey. Shame she never paid any attention to that kind of crap in the Brownies.

A lump of rusted twisty machinery loomed out of the forest, like the skeleton of a long-dead beast.

'SERGEANT MOORE!'

On. Deeper.

A noise up ahead.

Roberta hurried forward, struggling through a thicket of branches and brambles, out into a tiny clearing – no more than twenty foot across, knee-deep in sodden bracken. A stone circle festered in the middle of it. Not a big swanky photogenic one, like on *Outlander*, but a small mean one, with lichen-furred stones. The kind of place you could sacrifice children to the Elder Gods without waking the neighbours.

She stepped out from beneath the forest canopy into the proper rain. It drummed a tattoo on her high-vis shoulders.

Mountains reared up behind the woods, their top two-thirds lost in the grey misty clouds. Whole place couldn't be more remote and primeval if it tried.

'SERGEANT MOORE!'

Didn't matter how much she strained her ears, only the rain replied.

Maybe her voice wasn't carrying through the woods? What she needed was something to make bigger noises with...

Roberta picked up a fallen branch and whacked it against a thin beech tree at the edge of the clearing with a loud *clack*.

'SERGEANT—'

A whole heap of water cascaded from the tree's shaking leaves, most of which crashed down on top of her.

'Gah!'

She danced backwards, away from the deluge, but something grabbed the back of her heel and *crash*, she was flat on her back in the long wet bracken. Which promptly dumped another torrent of water all over her. Leaving Roberta lying there, looking up at the horrible grey clouds as four million litres of soggy soaked into her.

She'd got Sergeant Moore killed, hadn't she? She'd dragged him out here, into this bastarding forest, chasing a psycho, MP-murdering bastard, and got him *killed*. The whole thing was a piss-buggering disaster.

'AAAAAAAAAAAAAARGH!' Roberta scrambled to her feet, grabbed her branch and battered the living crap out of the traitorous beech tree with it. Whacking and thumping and howling with rage, because everything was comprehensively—

'Are you OK?'

She turned – branch still raised, ready for another wallop – and there was Sergeant Moore, limping out from behind a clump of brambles, one hand pressed against the small of his back, breathing hard.

Roberta waved her stick at him. 'Where the goat-*wanking* hell have you been?'

He pointed over his shoulder. 'I fell down a—'

'Had me worried sick! Sodding off on your own when there's a killer on the loose!'

Moore looked from her to the branch in her hand, then to

the beech she'd been beating to within an inch of its woody life. 'Did you think the *tree* did it?'

Roberta lowered her whacking stick. 'Don't be a—'

'Hope you read Mr Beech his rights before you embarked on the police brutality. Don't want Professional Standards coming after you.'

She treated him to a scowl. 'I liked it better when I thought you were dead.'

'Yeah, my ex-wife feels much the same way.'

The branch came up, indicating the general direction he'd emerged from. 'Anything?'

'Nah. Whoever it was, they're long gone.'

Of course they were.

Roberta slumped for a moment, then hurled her stick away into the forest. 'AAAAAAAAAAAAAAAAAAAAARGH!'

All this way, in the rain, for *nothing*.

She squelched across the hotel lawn, every step sounding like her socks were having extremely dirty sex with her shoes. And would it stop raining? Not a chance in hell.

Sergeant Moore limped beside her, grey hair plastered to his head, glasses all steamed up and covered in raindrops. 'So, were you really worried about me?'

'You got any idea how much paperwork they make you fill in for a dead sergeant?' Roberta pulled a face. 'No' to mention all the *meetings*.'

He thunked a hand down on her shoulder and squeezed. 'You old softie.'

'Hoy! Less of the "old". Bad enough we've got some nutter out in the woods playing Rambo, without me kicking your nadgers so hard they pop out your ears.'

'Ah.' The hand made a swift retreat. 'Fair enough. Back to interviewing Tories?'

'Do we have to?' Because it was enough to make you weep, it really was.

'You're Senior Investigating Officer: up to you.'

'I *hate* being the responsible adult.' She sagged a bit. 'Fine, we'll go talk to more Tories. But I'm getting dry socks on first!'

The bridal suite, AKA: 'Royal Lochnagar 1972', was so big it made the dodgy wee Russian's room look like a dog kennel that'd been decorated by someone who just didn't *love* tartan enough. Whoever committed interior design on this place *adored* the bloody stuff. A four-poster bed was visible through the open bedroom door, the canopy draped in Macdonald. Royal Stewart on the floor. A MacGregor couch and chaise longue, complete with Menzies, Wallace, and McLeod cushions.

To be brutally honest, the overall effect was a bit like standing inside a migraine.

Buchanan curtains framed the bay windows and a view that stretched all the way down a tree-lined avenue, past formal gardens, and out to the heather-wreathed hills. All of it draped in grey and rain and low, low clouds.

The bride and groom posed in front of the window, flanked by those headache-inducing swathes of yellow, orange, red, and green, as if they'd been caught in the middle of a photo-shoot. The pair of them in muted greys – probably scared of clashing with the décor.

Douglas Moore put a hand on his new wife's broad shoulder. 'It's been a terrible shock to us all, hasn't it, darling?'

Tears sparked in the corners of Adriana's eyes. 'One can

barely put into words the tragedy of losing one's father. *Complete* nightmarefest.'

Wonder if she'd kept her own name, taken his, or gone for the full triple-barrel? Bet that'd make ordering a takeaway pizza a right pain in the backside. By the time you'd spelled 'Adriana Bradbury-Scott-Moore' for the idiot on the other end of the phone, your twelve-inch meat feast would be cold.

Roberta sank onto the horrible chaise longue, wriggling her shoeless toes in their nice dry socks. And, OK, her jeans were still all soggy, but on the bright side they'd leave a nice damp patch on the ugly furniture. 'Our sympathies at this difficult time. Can you—'

'Not to mention the loss to his beloved Conservative Party!' Douglas gazed off into the middle distance, just the other side of a sparkly chandelier. 'He was a real *character*. A true one-nation Tory! To lose a stalwart MP like that and have to run a by-election in the current political climate?'

Adriana bit her lip and looked away. 'Hardly bears thinking about, yah?'

Sergeant Moore didn't seem to be writing any of this down. Instead he had this weird, someone's-just-stuffed-a-live-chicken-up-my-bum-and-I'm-not-enjoying-it look on his face. He cleared his throat, shuffled his bare feet. 'Dougie, surely there's more important—'

'I *may* have to give up my proposed seat and run in poor, *dear*, Sir Reginald's constituency instead.'

Adriana put her hand on her husband's arm. 'I think Daddy would like that, Douglas.'

A set of tiny wrinkles marred his photoshoot brow. 'Well, they say Aberdeen South's looking a bit marginal now, but the *important* thing is that Sir Reginald's constituents have someone to champion their causes. Fight for their rights.'

She blinked, nodded, and stepped in for an embrace.

Gazing up at the floppy-haired sockwank like he was the second sodding coming. 'We'll do it in his name.'

He looked deep into her eyes. 'In *his* name.'

To paraphrase that great wordsmith and renowned raconteur Adriana Bradbury-Scott-Moore: vomitarama!

Out in the corridor, Sergeant Moore eased the door closed, shutting the bride and groom in their horrible tartan love nest. He grimaced and marched off, not making eye contact. 'Before you say anything: don't, OK?'

She wandered after him, hands in her pockets. '"No" so much as a pause between, "Oh, it's such a tragedy" and "I'm nabbing his safe Tory seat."'

Moore paused, shoulders down, voice dark and bitter. 'Takes after his mother, that one.'

Roberta patted him on the back. 'You must be so proud.'

After the honeymoon suite, 'Strathisla' was a bit of a disappointment. Mind you, the décor in here was less likely to induce cluster headaches, vertigo, and nausea, so swings and roundabouts.

Mr Norton and his wife were in matching tweed. Which was quite something, given that it was absolutely *boiling* in their hotel room. What's worse, she was wearing a cardigan under her jacket too. A nasty thick yellow one.

They clung to each other like drowning, love-struck teenagers, albeit drowning love-struck teenagers with dangly wattle necks, liverspots, a bumper-selection-box of wrinkles, and yellowy-grey hair.

Mr Norton shook his head, setting his turkey neck wobbling. 'Oh, it was just *ghastly*, wasn't it, Catherine? Simply *ghastly*.'

Mrs Norton nodded, tears sparkling in her boiled-egg eyes. 'He was such a card, he really was. We'll miss him terribly.'

Roberta sagged against the balcony handrail, scowling down at the tartan carpet and that stupid massive stag statue. Supposed to be a romantic surprise break, and now look at it – blood-crusted antlers and a hotel full of angry Tory scumbags, whinging because *apparently* being confined to your room was worse than having to investigate a murder.

Sergeant Moore settled in next to her. 'Well, it's early days, right?'

That familiar gurgling growl rumbled away inside her, like distant hungry thunder. Ending with a couple of pops and a wheezing sound. 'Time is it?'

He checked. 'Just gone five.'

And nothing to eat since brunchtime. 'No wonder I'm starving.'

'Seventeen interviews down, twenty-nine to go.'

'Gah... Told you we'd be here all weekend.'

Six hours of interrogating smug Tory bastards, and not a single clue to show for it. Oh, he was such a lovely man, so good with children, a great chap, did so much work for charity, salt of the earth. Blowing smoke up a corpse's arse was second nature to these people.

But that's what an expensive private education got you, wasn't it? None of the buggers could think for themselves. It was all stock phrases and platitudes. Or maybe it was secret Tory code for something – like with dating profiles, where 'great sense of humour', meant 'fat', and 'bubbly personality', meant '*enormously* fat'. So, in Toryspeak, 'Oh, he's a real character' probably meant 'he's a bit of a dick'; 'such a card' meant 'tosser'; and 'salt of the earth' was 'complete and utter total wankspasm'.

Would make life a lot easier if they'd just come out and say it.

Sergeant Moore sniffed. 'What do you want to do?'

'Gin. Tonic. And enough chips to choke a goat. With cheese and gravy...' Her stomach growled again. 'Come on. Can't catch killers on an empty stomach.'

12

Apparently, the 'swanky tartan' budget didn't extend to the staff quarters. There weren't even any stuffed animal heads on the walls, just lots of magnolia paint, with a poopy shade of brown below a rubber dado rail. Grey carpet tiles, a bit curly at the edges, and patched in places with silver duct tape. The kind of motivational posters that should get middle-management-types done for crimes against humanity. 'EVERY DAY YOU DO YOUR BEST IS A GREAT DAY!', 'GET OUT THERE AND SHOW THE WORLD WHAT YOU CAN DO!', and Roberta's personal favourite: 'A SMILE MAKES EVERYONE'S DAY – BE SOMEONE'S REASON TO SMILE TODAY!' Which, for some unfathomable reason, came with a photo of a piglet in a propeller beanie.

Roberta raised a fist and gave the door marked 'HOTEL CHEF' three knocks, loud and hard. Opened it without waiting for an answer and stuck her head in. 'Hoy, Raymond Blanc, you're up.'

It was an OK room, as rooms went. Nowhere near as large as the guests' ones, and without any of the fancy fixtures and fittings. The six-foot fat man pacing up and down the carpet tiles, smoking up a storm, didn't help it feel any bigger. His chef's checked trousers looked about ready to burst, held up by a pair of red-white-and-blue braces. A sweaty red T-shirt and jaunty white neckerchief. A cliché of French posters graced the walls: the Arc de Triomphe, Eiffel Tower, Toulouse-Lautrec's can-can girls, blocks of cheese, and big bottles of wine... But the end wall was solid bookshelves, overflowing with cookery books.

The hotel chef didn't stop pacing as he glared at her on the way past, a Gauloise sticking out the corner of his rubbery-lipped mouth – the strong distinctive white smoke curling up around the waxed handlebars of his little moustache. As if Hercule Poirot had swallowed a minibus. 'Ow am I supposed to prepare dinner if I am cooped up in 'ere?' He waved his cigarette at her as he turned and paced past again. 'I 'ave no fresh delivery, I 'ave people to feed that should not be 'ere, but nothing to feed them *weeth*, there is dirty-big padlock on my fridge,' he paused just long enough to stamp his foot, 'and I am stuck in this son-of-bitch room!'

Roberta smiled at him. 'Oh, I'm sure we can work something out.'

For an overstuffed fat man, he was surprisingly light on his feet, pirouetting from fridge to stove to worktop and back again in a strange mesmerising wobbly ballet. His white chef's jacket stretched tight across that massive belly.

He battered a net of carrots down on the stainless steel in front of him. 'Zees is intolerable! It eez *impossible* to create ze culinary masterpiece for forty guests from nothing!'

Sergeant Moore flipped the page in his notebook. 'Can we just get back to the subject in hand, please? Did you see anyone arguing or fighting with Sir Reginald?'

'Carrots! All I have is carrots and what you Scottish call, "neeeeps". *Sacrebleu!*'

'Did you see anyone arguing or fighting with—'

'Merde!' The chef ripped the carrot bag open and dug out a fat handful. 'A six-course meal is not something you can throw together with carrots and neeeeps!'

'Did – you – see – anyone—'

'I 'ave worked in two-Michelin star restaurants! I 'ave made demi-glace that would cause the Holy Father to weep for its beauty!'

Moore bit his top lip and turned to Roberta. 'Honestly, I can't—'

A pot slammed down next to the carrots. 'CARROTS AND NEEEEPS! Where does that feature in Escoffier's books?'

She tilted her head on one side. There was something ... off about that statement. Something weird and out of place.

'I 'ave a reputation to maintain! I am ze great Gérard de Larosière of Skirivour Castle Hotel, not some *Greasy Reechard at Leetle Chef!*' He yanked a peeler from a drawer and set about his carrots. It was like watching a race car whizz past, he was that quick, denuding the pointy orange lumps and hurling them into the pot.

Sergeant Moore rapped his knuckles against the worktop. 'Look, are you going to answer the bloody question or not?'

She leaned back against the stove and raised an eyebrow at him. 'More importantly, are you going to tell us who you *really* are?'

The chef paused in his peeling, then went back to it at Formula 1 pace. 'I told you: I am ze great—'

'Only, your French accent's a bit OTT, isn't it? A bit put-on.'

His rosy cheeks flushed a darker shade. 'Ow *dare* you eensult my noble—'

'Say, "book" again.'

He grabbed another handful of carrots. 'I don't 'ave time for zees, I 'ave dinner to prepare.'

'Go on, "Gérard", *humour* me.'

A theatrical sigh. Then, 'Book.'

And there it was.

'See? You're about as French as my knickers. It's pronounced "book", no' "boo-wke". That's pure Brummie that is.'

Gérard stared at her, eyes wide, mouth an open, quivering pink hole. Then he licked his lips. Looked left and right. Waddled to the kitchen door and poked his head out into the dining room. Came back again. And this time, his accent was one hundred percent made-in-Birmingham. 'Yow can't tell anyone, roight? I've made me livin' out of being French. You sound like this, no one takes you seriously in a professional kitchen. You gorra be French to werk in a five-star hotel.'

Roberta pointed at Moore's notebook. 'Name?'

'Nah, it really is "Gérard de Larosière". Changed it by deed poll from Tony Heppelthwaite.'

'All right, Tony, here's the deal: you want to keep on being French, that's fine with me. Couldn't give a monkey's hairy toss. But you don't tell us everything we want to know – and I mean *everything* – you're up the Grand Union Canal without a paddle.'

He deflated a bit, shrinking by at least two inches. Then nodded. 'Go on, then.'

Sergeant Moore had another go. 'Did you see anyone fighting or arguing with Sir Reginald?'

'To his *face*? Naw. Everyone acts like his farts smell of Malibu-and-Coke to his face. Behind his back, though? Surprised he could sleep lying down for all the knives in it.'

'Anyone in particular?'

'Now yer askin'. See, he didn't do himself no favours with this goldmine thing.'

Roberta ran a finger along the cooker controls. Keeping her voice all light and innocent. 'You had money in his investment scheme?'

'Investment *scam*, more like.' The bitterness positively dripped from his voice. 'I was savin' up for me own place – nice little B&B. Do me own meals and that. Just me and me mate, Baz. Well, *boyfriend*.' Gérard leaned forwards on the countertop, gesturing with the peeler. 'I wanna get married, but he won't commit, you know? Only Sir Reginald Bradbury-Bleedin'-Scott talks us into sinking most of our stake into this goldmine he's frontin'. Gonna make a fortune, ain't we?' For a moment, Gérard inflated … then deflated again. 'Only it didn't werk like that. Turns out the guy *runnin'* the goldmine's wanted on an international arrest warrant and the National Crime Agency's seizing all his assets. And that means all *our* money.'

He stared at the pile of unpeeled carrots in front of him, grabbed the knife and hacked at them with bared teeth and homicidal abandon. Dumped the knife and grabbed a meat-tenderising hammer from the drawer, whacking away till there was nothing but bright orange mush left.

Puffing and panting, he put the hammer down again and pulled on a posh voice. '"So sorry, old bean," says Sir Reg, "it's completely out of my hands. I had simply *no idea* he was a bad egg."' Back to normal for, 'Yeah, right. Bet he got to keep his commission, though.'

Roberta sighed. 'The rich get richer.'

'And the poor saps like us get screwed over. Every single time.' Gérard leaned forward again. 'You know, I know I shouldn't say it, cos you're the bizzies and everything, but I'm *glad* he's dead. Waltzing round here, like there's a silver spoon up his arse and he's doin' us a favour lettin' us sniff it.' Gérard marched over to the fridge and returned with a net of neeps. Dug one out and bashed it down on the chopping board. 'Come the revolution?' The knife whistled down, bisecting the neep neatly in two.

Sergeant Moore raised a fist in salute. 'Right on, comrade.'

And Gérard pulled the same face he'd done when Roberta rumbled him for an undercover Brummie. 'I'm norra bleedin' *Communist*! I voted Conservative last five general elections, thank you very much.'

'But—'

'We're nor all toffee-nosed tossers, you know! Some of us believe in small government, personal responsibility, and people actually werkin' for a living.' Another neep got its napper cleaved in two. Then Gérard went a bit misty-eyed, staring off into space. 'What amma gonna do about dinner? There's leftovers from the weddin', but someone's been *at* those. You should see the state of that roast beef – looks like a wolverine's been chewin' it.'

Sergeant Moore took a sudden interest in his notebook.

Roberta cleared her throat and picked at her fingernails.

Yeah...

She put on that innocent voice again. 'I wouldn't mind a slice or three?'

'Had to chuck it in the bin. It's not *hygienic*, you see. Don't even know if the thieving bastard washed his hands ferst! I serve that, and give half the local Conservative Party botulism, I'm out on me arse.'

'Oh.' What a waste of lovely pink beef. They should've scarfed the lot this morning and no one would've been any the wiser. 'Er... Nothing in the freezer?'

'Naaaaah. Well, haunch of venison, but it won't defrost in...' A smile bloomed on his chubby face, making his eyes almost disappear in the folds. 'That's *bostin*'! I'll give Albert a shout: he can nip out and shoot summit for us.'

Roberta and Moore raised their eyebrows at each other.

'Albert?'

'You know: the gamekeeper-slash-handyman? Albert Nairn? Old bloke, nose like a shark humping a sack of wrinkles?'

'Ah.' The tweedy old man who'd found her in the long grass that morning.

'I know we're all *meant* to be confined to barracks, but you'd let him out to shoot somethin' for dinner, wouldn't yez? I mean, it's not like anyone'd notice he'd gone, is it? How could you tell?'

Sergeant Moore looked up from scribbling in his book. 'How could we tell?'

'Well, he doesn't live in the hotel, does he? Lucky sod's gorra tied cottage in the woods. Can come and go as he pleases and who'd ever know?'

The mysterious stranger who disappeared into the woods: it was the bloody gamekeeper, out and about when he should've been in and not.

'Tell you what, let us know how to find his cottage and we'll go ask him for you.' Roberta pushed off from the stovetop. 'Sergeant Moore can take the details.'

Took a while, but eventually the chef had sketched out a passable map in Moore's notebook, complete with arrows and dotted lines and things.

Soon as it was done, Gérard went back to his *'Allo 'Allo* accent. 'Zut alors, madame gendarme, eet 'as been my pleasure!' Then he grabbed her hand, bent, and kissed it.

Urgh...

It was like being tongued by a slug.

Roberta *vwwwwwwipp*ed up her high-vis's zip and stood, staring through the hotel's front doors at the miserable rain. The puddles out there had spread and deepened, the sky darkened to bruised concrete. They'd have to build an ark at this rate.

Sergeant Moore struggled into his fluorescent-yellow jacket, pulling a face. 'Is yours all clammy? Mine is all clammy.'

Yeah. And so were her socks – the water leeching out of her squelchy trainers right through to her rapidly wrinkling toes. Trousers *still* hadn't dried out either. Going to catch her death of mildew at this rate.

A rumble of thunder growled in the distance.

'Sounds like my stomach.' She produced a pilfered carrot from her pocket and crunched off a bite.

'Going to get soaked, aren't we?'

Crunch, chew, chew, chew. 'Already done that *three times* today. Don't fancy another go.'

Moore had a rummage behind the reception desk, coming out with a little photocopied map. 'You think it might be him? Our killer?'

'With this lot? Might be anyone.' She cracked off another carroty nugget. 'If he's the gamekeeper-slash-handyman, he'd know where those big ladders were, wouldn't he?'

Moore nodded. 'Yup.'

'He comes and goes as he pleases, has access to weapons, and I bet he's got keys to every room in the hotel too. In case they need fixing. I'd say he had to be pretty high up the suspect list.'

Sergeant Moore plucked a couple of hotel brollies from the stand by the doors and stepped out onto the gravel beneath the portico, skirting one of those spreading puddles in his sodden socks and soggy shoes. 'Shame you didn't bring the wellington boots in from the Landy. Would've come in handy right about now.'

She stared at him. 'I traipsed across half the Highlands in my only dry shoes, and there were *wellies* in the Land Rover?'

That was it, it was official now: next time she got her hands on PC McKinnon, she was going to bloody well kill him.

Fifteen minutes from the hotel and the woods thickened around them like something out of the Brothers Grimm. Dark and damp and deep, the canopy filtering-down the never-ending rain to plops and dribbles that pattered into the leaf litter coating the gloomy forest floor.

And, swear to God, it felt like the trees were watching them. Tiny little eyes in the darkness, staring as they made their way along the winding path, past jagged tangles of barbed-wire brambles and great drooping ferns.

Every now and then a drip would thunk into the fabric of her brolly, reverberating unnaturally loud in the arboreal silence.

Something *clicked* in the undergrowth – off to the right, where the shadows had congealed to almost total darkness – and Roberta froze. Beside her, Sergeant Moore did the same, and they stood there, listening. And listening. And listening.

Just the patter of those filtered raindrops.

Moore's voice was barely a whisper: 'You ever see *The Deer Hunter*?'

'More like bloody *Deliverance*.'

What if it was Nairn, the gamekeeper? Out there stalking them like they were a couple of deer. Just waiting for the best time to start shooting...

A minute passed. Then another one.

OK, they weren't dead yet, so it probably wasn't him. Just a badger or something. Nothing to worry about.

Ahem.

She hurried on, following the path. 'So, a wee birdie tells me your ex-wife liked to put it about a bit?'

You could tell Moore was forcing the words out between gritted teeth, they had that kind of strangled sound. 'I'm *not* talking about this.'

'Come on, tell your Aunty Roberta all about it.' Because someone else's troubles were always a lot more fun than your own.

'And you can tell Constable Michael McKinnon, next time he shoots his mouth off about my personal life I'm going to park that Land Rover up his backside!' And with that, Sergeant Moore marched off at double speed, leaving her behind. Cos Susan wasn't the only world-class sulker.

Roberta stood there, grinning as his high-vis figure got smaller. 'WAS IT SOMETHING I SAID?'

'You sure we're no' just going round and round in circles?'

Sergeant Moore slogged on. 'Maybe?'

If anything, the woods had got darker and deeper. The path had narrowed too, reducing them to shuffling along in single file. Moore in the front, Roberta bringing up the rear.

'If there's no gingerbread cottage at the end of this, I'm going to be really hacked off.'

He paused and checked their sketched map. 'Should be round about here, somewhere…'

And on they squelched.

Moore looked over his shoulder at her. 'You done many of these? Murder inquiries?'

'Millions of them. Well, at least fourteen, anyway. Maybe sixteen? Kinda lose count after a while.'

'Wow.' Genuinely looking impressed.

'You hear about the Flesher case? I worked that.'

'*Seriously?*'

'Couldn't eat sausages for a month. Absolute torture.'

The path jinked around to the right, and as they followed it the woods opened out into a clearing of ropey grass dotted with the stumps of long-dead trees – their dark bloated wood peppered with pale pustulant mushrooms.

Sergeant Moore just stood there at the edge of the clearing, mouth hanging open.

Couldn't blame him. Because if you were looking for grade-A creepy, this was the mother lode. A cottage sat in the middle of the clearing, its steep roof sagging around a stone chimney – pale smoke curling away into the low grey cloud. Mean little windows glowered out from beneath the eaves, the wooden cladding festered with lichen. It looked … *malevolent*. Like the kind of place a serial killer would skin his victims. Then eat them.

A porch ran along the front, complete with rocking chair. A wood shed caught in the act of slow-motion collapse. What was probably an outhouse just visible at the back of the mouldy property.

But that wasn't what made Roberta stare. It was the bones. Big bones. Small bones. Some on their own, some joined together in bundles. Here and there they made an almost complete skeleton – skull, spine, ribs, and pelvis, with only the limbs missing. Deer, dogs, badgers, you name it. All trussed up and dangling from metal poles driven into the clearing floor.

She huffed out a breath. 'Wow… Talk about a "fixer-upper".'

'Or a "stay-the-hell-away-from-er".'

13

The path snaked its way between the bone offerings to the cottage's ratty wooden porch.

Roberta grimaced. 'Aye ... don't know about you but I'm promoting our sinister gamekeeper to Suspect Number One.'

'Right.' Moore squared his shoulders. 'Let's go rattle the bugger's cage.' He marched along the path, back straight, head up. Hotel umbrella held high and proud.

She stayed where she was, watching him go.

This, right here, was the start of pretty much every horror movie that ended up with everyone dead and eaten. And she was far too pretty to end up in some fusty old git's casserole dish.

But it wasn't as if Sergeant Moore could cope on his own, was it? Man was about as useful as a chocolate soup bowl.

Which meant, like it or not, she had to follow the daft bugger into the monster's lair.

'Bah.' She squelched along after him, rain thuddering against her brolly, cascading off the brim in teeny waterfalls.

Up ahead, Sergeant Moore came to a complete halt halfway down the path, as bottle-tops and empty tins rattled on either side of him. Was that a *tripwire* wrapped around his left ankle?

Yeah, that wasn't suspicious *at all*.

He backed away a couple of paces, shaking his foot free of the line. 'Maybe we should—'

The cottage door banged open and the gamekeeper stepped out, face a collection of hard angry wrinkles, the shotgun pointing right at them. 'What do *you* want?'

Roberta picked her way past Moore – putting herself between him and the gun – and treated the old psycho to a nice unthreatening smile. 'Albert? Albert Nairn? Police.' Just so there was no confusion, she grabbed Sergeant Moore's shoulders and spun him around to show off the word 'POLICE' picked out in reflective silver letters on the back of his high-vis jacket.

Nairn raised a hairy grey eyebrow. 'Oh aye?'

'Any chance we can come in out of the pishing rain? Only I left my gills at home.'

He narrowed his eyes, mouth pinched like he was trying to suck something out of his dentures. Then he harrumphed, turned, and headed back inside, leaving the door open behind him.

Moore turned the right way around again. 'Bet he's got a banjo in there.'

'At least he didn't tell you you've got a pretty mouth.' She climbed up onto the porch and stepped inside.

OK, that was ... different.

The cottage was all one room, with a bed in the corner, a rocking chair by the fireplace, and a kitchen table with three wooden seats. No TV, no radio. A trio of storm lanterns hung from hooks in the ceiling, lending the place a septic-yellow glow that wasn't anywhere near bright enough to banish the gloom. But more than enough to really add to the horror-show vibe Albert Nairn was clearly going for.

There were probably more dead things in this one room than there were in the whole of Skirivour Castle Hotel. Only where the hotel's collection of taxidermy was fairly standard, the stuffed menagerie in here was a lot more ... *creative*. And less bound by anatomical and evolutionary constraints.

Every wall was lined with shelves, and shelves, and shelves, all groaning under the weight of dead things in various stages of finish. More hung from the ceiling, between the lanterns.

Albert Nairn had let his imagination run rampant. One ceiling-dangling monstrosity was part fox, part hare, and part badger. A salmon-squirrel hybrid stared at Roberta from its shelf, with glittering black-glass eyes. What *probably* used to be a border collie had been merged with a goat and an eagle... And there were dozens and dozens of other pick-'n'-mix monsters: all different, all weird.

He'd arranged some in semi-natural poses – or whatever passed for semi-natural when you had the back end of a wildcat, the front end of a fawn, and the head of a duck – but the *really* freaky chimeras were the ones doing people things. Strange day-to-day tableaus, like the half-raven-half-stoat, wearing a tartan miniskirt and loading a miniature tumble drier.

Roberta blinked at it for a bit. But it really *was* there, stuffing teeny red socks into the machine. 'OK...'

Nairn gave her another harrumph, propped his shotgun against the wall, and sat at the rickety table with his back to her. Fiddling away at something.

Sergeant Moore slipped in from outside and closed the door. Then stood there, gawping at Dr Moreau's petting zoo. 'Well, this is ... *homely*.'

'Hmph.'

'We need to have a word.' Roberta ducked under a twelve-legged foxipede, on her way to the table.

Soon as she drew level with it, Nairn slid an empty chair out for her with his foot – the wooden legs screeching across the bare floorboards.

She settled into it. 'So, Albert. Bert. Bertie?'

He fixed her with his yellowy eyes. '"Nairn" is fine.'

'Right, *Nairn*, we need to talk to you about…' And that's when it finally registered what the old man was actually working on. 'Oh.'

It was a tableau of the morning's jolly discovery, rendered in weird-as-hell taxidermy. He'd replaced the stag statue with a stuffed squirrel. Only the squirrel had little antlers and hooves on its back legs. The part of Sir Reginald Bradbury-Scott was played by a mouse, impaled on the squirrel's 'antlers', just like the real-life version. The mouse was even wearing a teeny pair of tartan pyjamas – the bottoms down around its ankles.

Nairn turned his creation, so she could get a good long look at it. 'Lot of people'll tell you about the Jackalope, but that's a Yank creature.' He pointed at the squirrel-thing with a strange mixture of pride and awe in his voice. '*Feòrag a 'Bhàis* stalks the glens and moors of Scotland, and if he catches your soul when you die, before you can flee this filthy world, he buries it beneath an ancient oak tree, where the twisted roots will feast on it and claim you as their own.'

'*Right.*' Mad as a sack of hedgehogs. She shared a quick look with Sergeant Moore, trying not to make it too obvious. 'And did you make this today? Because it's a lot of work since this morning.'

A smile blossomed on that wrinkly face, followed a moment later by a high ringing laugh as Nairn swung a finger up, pointing at a shelf behind her.

And when she turned, there they were: a whole chorus line of antlered squirrels, all just waiting their turn to shine in some exciting frieze.

He lowered the finger. 'Now *this* was more challenging.' Bending over, he guddled about under the table, emerging with a small wooden box about the size of a cigarette packet.

He lifted the lid and pulled out another mouse. This one was white, wearing blue trousers and teeny stripy red-and-black socks. And a grey bra that was a pretty accurate representation of Old Faithful. The mouse even had a miniature chamber pot in one hand.

He'd made a little her. A dead mouse mini-me.

'Eeek...'

'Had to glue three kinds of badger fur to its head to get the hair right.' Nairn stroked the shock of greys up into random spikes, then placed Rodent Roberta on the table in front of her. It stood there – or at least balanced on its own two ... paws – looking up at her with shiny glass eyes.

'Well, that's just... It's... I...'

His voice softened, like an indulgent uncle. 'You can keep her if you like. I can always make another.'

She stared at the mouse, then at Sergeant Moore, then at Albert Nairn, then back to Moore again, eyebrows creeping further and further up her head. *Help!*

Moore took out his notebook. 'Mr Nairn, you were familiar with Sir Reginald Bradbury-Scott, were you not?' All formal.

The smile vanished from Nairn's face. 'Never does to be *familiar* with the aristocracy, they don't like it when the lower classes get ideas above their station.'

Roberta blinked.

Did she really look like that?

I mean, it was flattering ... in a *way*. A very weird and disturbing way, but still.

'I take it you didn't like him very much?'

'Oh, the man was an absolute shite, but that's his prerogative as a knight of the realm.' Nairn went into his toolbox for a sort of hooked tool, a saucer, and another mouse – a fresh one this time. Digging away at its insides. Making sticky red screlchy noises. 'Not my business to like him or not.'

No one had ever made a taxidermied statue of her before. Or if they had, they'd kept it to themselves.

'Where were you last night between the hours of eleven and six a.m.?'

'It's the natural order of things, isn't it? Some folks is above other folks, some folks is beneath.' He pointed a chunk of hooked-out mouse at another shelf. 'Your sea eagle eats the fox, the fox eats the weasel, the weasel eats the mouse, the mouse eats worms and bugs. There's an *order*, it's how nature works.' More digging.

Roberta shook her head, breaking eye contact with the teeny her. 'Aye, but only because the worms can't take up arms and overthrow their sea eagle oppressors.' A frown. 'Because they haven't *got* any arms.' Looking around at the cut-and-paste-animal horror show. 'Not yet, anyway.'

'Mr Nairn, I need to know where you were between eleven last night and six this morning.'

A chunk of innards splotched into the saucer. 'Does a body good to know who his betters are.'

'Nah.' She settled back in her seat. 'The class system exists for one reason and one reason only: to keep people like you and me down. And it only works because dafties buy into the fiction that some buggers really *are* inherently better than others just because of who their mum and dad are. It's like Tinkerbell: only exists if you believe in it.'

Sergeant Moore put his pen down. 'Is anyone listening to me at all?'

'Clap if you believe in the upper classes, children!'

Nairn gave a long, slow clap. 'And don't pretend you're *anything* like me. You're not working class.'

Roberta stiffened. 'Don't tell me I'm no' working—'

'You're a *detective chief inspector*. You told the Laird to go to his room, and he did. You think someone "working class" could do that?' Nairn pointed his hook at the shelf again. 'You're not a sea eagle, but maybe you're a fox or a weasel?' He narrowed his eyes. 'Or mebby a grey wolf.' Back to digging. 'Me and Sergeant Moore here? We're worms.'

'Speak for yourself.' Moore chapped on the tabletop. 'Now, where the hell were you last night?'

Nairn pulled the last gobbet of innards from his mouse and wiped the hook clean on his sleeve. 'Once the wedding guests had gone, I stacked all the chairs in the ballroom and came home.' His eyes drifted over Sergeant Moore's shoulder. 'Been working on a special project and wanted to get the ears done.'

Somehow that managed to sound even creepier than everything else.

Roberta turned in her seat and stopped.

OK... Just when you thought Albert Nairn couldn't get any odder.

A hideous man-animal thing lurked in the shadows beside a bookcase full of owl parts. It was only about a third finished, but the framework had to be *at least* six foot six. God knew how many species had contributed to the repulsive melange, but it was a lot of them. Stag's antlers reached up from either side of its head, with curling ram's horns beneath them, spines of bone making a line down its back. There was something primitive about it. Something that made the air taste metallic and *greasy* all at the same time. Nairn hadn't got around to putting the eyes in yet, but the empty sockets of whatever he'd used for the skull still stared back at her. Hostile and judging.

A shudder rippled its way across her shoulders, making the hair on her arms stick up.

Whatever the hell Nairn was making, it was wrong in *so* many ways.

That strange pride-and-awe sound was back in the old freak's voice. 'Cernunnos: the Horned God!' A happy sigh. 'The secret is to use only the *freshest* of roadkill.'

Roberta dragged her gaze back to the table. 'Did you kill Sir Reginald Bradbury-Scott?'

'Pff...' He picked up a short-bladed knife. 'Worms don't kill eagles. They get eaten and are thankful for it.'

Roberta huddled under her hotel umbrella, peering back across the clearing at Albert Nairn's Cottage of Horrors. The mini-me-mouse version of her was soft and furry against her fingers as she stroked it in her pocket. Which sounded like a filthy euphemism, but it was kinda weirdly comforting. Soothing, even.

Look: here's a dead rodent that's been dressed up to look *just* like me.

Wasn't every day you got to say something like that.

Sergeant Moore sidled up beside her, the rain drumming on his umbrella. 'What do you think?'

'Creepy as a creepy thing.'

'Oh *hell* yes. But did he do it?'

'Don't know... Maybe.' She frowned at all those bones, hanging from their metal posts. Couldn't deny that the whole place screamed SERIAL KILLER! in six-foot-tall neon letters, decorated with dead mix-and-match animals, but just because the guy was a grade-A nutbasket, it didn't make him a killer, did it? 'Displaying the body like that, up on the stag's horns? *That* I can see him doing.'

'OK.' Moore pulled his shoulders back, chin up, being all heroic. 'Want me to go in there and arrest him? Got to be a room at the hotel we could lock him in till Inverness gets here.'

'Thought you didn't have handcuffs with you?'

'Ah...'

Roberta grabbed the sleeve of his high-vis and dragged him further into the woods, behind a thicket of brambles. Which, if they were lucky, would offer a bit of camouflage. Difficult to be sneaky in an oversized fluorescent-yellow waterproof and a bright-blue brolly with 'Skirivour Castle Hotel' on it.

He hunkered beside her, keeping his voice down. 'It was Nairn running around in the woods earlier, wasn't it?'

'Bloody well hope so. Wouldn't want *two* sinister-spooky sods messing about out here.'

Moore tried on a thinky face. 'Mind you, would a raving monarchist really kill someone like—'

'Shh!'

The cottage's door swung open and Albert Nairn stepped out onto the porch. He was wearing some sort of hairy cloak over his tweeds, stitched together from patchwork animal pelts. It had a rack of half-sized antlers mounted on either side of the hood, making him look like a dressing-up-box version of the monstrosity he was building in his cottage: Cernunnos.

Only the Horned God probably wasn't depicted holding a rifle big enough to stop an elephant. Assuming there were any roaming this part of the Scottish Highlands. Which was doubtful, because if there *were*, Nairn would have shot and stuffed one by now.

Moore ducked down. 'He knows we're on to him!'

She slapped his arm, voice a hissing whisper. 'Will you shut your hole?'

But Nairn didn't march over and blow a mammoth-sized

hole in either of them. Instead he stepped out into the rain, sniffing the air as he did a slow three-sixty. Then froze, hunkered down, and hurried off in the opposite direction, rifle held across his chest.

Roberta breathed out. 'See? He's no' coming after us.'

'Unless he's circling round behind…'

Now *there* was a comforting thought.

But no point standing here like a pair of lemons, waiting to find out if Moore was right or not.

Time to beat a hasty retreat.

Amazing how much ground you could cover when you thought a homicidal maniac was chasing after you.

Roberta and Sergeant Moore staggered in through the hotel entrance, puffing and panting. Thunking the doors shut behind them and shooting the bolts. Which probably wouldn't stop Nairn and his dirty-big rifle for long, but it was the thought that counted.

The lobby was silent and empty, just the dead animals and that massive stag statue to witness them kid-on they hadn't been running scared from an auld mannie in a hairy cloak.

She pushed herself off the door and had a wee shake, sending water spattering off her high-vis. Every step made horrible squishing noises. 'Feet are like sponges.'

Moore unzipped his soggy jacket and hung it on the rack. 'On the *plus* side, at least we've not been shot.'

'Know what? I get the feeling that if our boy Nairn *had* killed Sir Reginald, he'd have wheeched the body back to his weirdy cottage and stuffed it.' Roberta squelched in place for a couple of steps as she peeled off her waterproof. 'Never been so damp in my life. Aye, and that includes in the bath.' She pulled off her trainers and tipped the water out onto the tartan carpet. 'Haven't got a single dry sock to my name!'

Sergeant Moore put their umbrellas away. 'Actually ... I *think* there's something we can do about that.'

14

At least the hotel laundry didn't have a stupid whisky name.

Wooden shelves wrapped around three sides of the room, stacked high with bed linen, towels, and the rest of that housekeeping malarkey. A couple of massive tumble driers sat against the other wall, *whurrrrrrr*ing and rumbling, each one easily large enough to take a family of four – if you didn't mind squishing the children up a bit – leaving the middle of the room to a bank of industrial-strength washing machines that chugged, sloshed, and whirred as the weird ginger woman in the tartan miniskirt ironed her way through a stack of pillow cases. Doing her best not to look at the half-naked police officers loitering in her place of work.

Roberta wrapped the edge of the sheet around herself again, covering Old Faithful's straps. Didn't want Sergeant Moore getting all hot and bothered. That was the trouble with these heterosexual men: no self-control when it came to a flash of sexy flesh.

He didn't seem very comfortable in his sheet, shifting and fidgeting with it – like anyone was interested in his scabby blue Markie's pants and hairy knees – as he tried to take notes at the same time.

You know, with the pair of them done up in their DIY togas, and the weird woman in her short skirt, the laundry room kinda resembled a really badly organised Roman orgy, where no one remembered to bring any booze. Or butt plugs.

Their hostess finished ironing one pillowcase, folded it, and started on another. 'Oh, Sir Reginald was quite the *regular* here.' A sigh – both wistful and sad. 'Lovely man. Tipped really well.' She wiped a wee tear from her eye. 'All the staff loved him.'

'Oh aye?' Roberta leaned back against a washing machine as it *whirrrr*ed into its spin cycle, the whole thing vibrating enough make the floor judder. Like a huge, rectangular, stainless-steel sex toy.

Roberta's voice came out all wobbly as the machine really got into the throb of things. 'Then how come he came off as such a prick?'

'Oh, that was just his way. He was lovely, deep down. A proper gentleman.' She pointed the iron at them. 'You know what he was?'

'If you say "salt of the earth", "such a card", or "a real character" I'm going to cram that ironing board right up your laundry chute.'

Her cheeks flushed hot pink, clashing with her freckles and hair. 'Charming, I'm sure!'

Moore fiddled with his sheet again. 'What about Albert Nairn?'

'The gamekeeper?' She puffed out a breath. 'Now you're asking. He's quite good on washing machines, but hopeless with the rumblers.' Nodding at the two huge monstrosities as Roberta's trainers boinged and clonked, churning round and round and round...

'Did he have a problem with Sir Reginald?'

'What, like did they *fight* or something?' A laugh. 'God, can you imagine?' On to the next pillowcase. 'Anyway, Old Nairny wouldn't do anything that'd hurt His Lordship. Totally devoted, so he is. It's sweet, really. *Killing* a guest? God knows what the TripAdvisor reviews are going to be like after *this* weekend.' She put on a mock-posh voice. '"Lovely food and excellent service, but our stay was somewhat marred by the father-of-the-bride getting crucified in the lobby: three stars."'

'Damn it.' Sergeant Moore fumbled with his notebook and one side of his sheet slipped, exposing a nipple and the tattoo above — a skull and dagger with a woman's name wrapped around it on a scroll. Only the name had been scored out with a thick red line that looked a lot fresher than the faded blue-grey of the original design. 'Sorry.' He hauled the sheet back into place. 'Nairn's never threatened Sir Reginald in any way?'

'Don't be silly.'

The giant driers went *ding* and stopped turning.

Little Miss Miniskirt marched over there and pulled open both doors, letting out the warm fluffy scent of freshly tumbled clothes. 'There you go, all nice and dry and toasty.' She dug Roberta's T-shirt, jeans, socks, and trainers from the drum. 'Do you want them ironed?'

'Oh, no. I love it when they're still warm from the machine.' Roberta took the lot from her, holding the bundle close. Mmmmm, fuzzy loveliness. 'Sergeant Moore, you can either face the wall, cover your eyes, or get a knee in the nadgers.'

'Oh, not this again.' He turned to face the wall.

Roberta stuck her clothes on top of the ironing board and, as a special treat, gave the weird ginger woman a saucy wink and a good hard flash of Old Faithful. Something sexy for her to think about next time she was doing a big wash and the machines hit the spin cycle.

Never let it be said that Roberta Steel didn't do her bit for morale.

'Sorry, *again*.' Sergeant Moore waved at the weird woman and eased the laundry door closed, shutting her inside. Leaving him and Roberta outside in a bland magnolia corridor with pipes running along the ceiling. He'd ditched the toga for his now-dry clothes, shoes clutched in one hand and full of scrunched-up newspapers. Frowning at Roberta as she wriggled from side to side. 'Was that really necessary?'

'Mmmmm…' Eyes half-closed in bliss as the tumble-drier warmth seeped into her.

'Did you *have* to traumatise the poor woman?'

'I love jeans straight out the tumble drier – all nice and toasty on your bum and bits.'

Cheeky sod pretended to have a wee dry-boak at the image. Then: 'So, what do you want to do? More interviews, or—'

'Hoy!' She thumped him. 'One of life's little pleasures that is: toasty bits.'

He retreated out of bashing range and checked his notebook. 'So far, we've done eight couples and four singles, including our weird friend the animal-stuffer. That leaves seventeen guests and nine hotel staff to go.'

Roberta sagged a bit and frowned at him. 'You're harshing my mellow again, Sergeant.'

'We could do another three interviews, and that would make it halfway?'

'Sod that.' Roberta had one last toasty wriggle. 'Been ages since brunch and I'm starving. I don't get fed soon I'm going to hunt one of your Tories down and eat them.'

Bangs, clangs, and sizzling filled the kitchen, accompanied by great gouts of steam as Gérard de Larosière, AKA: Tony Heppelthwaite, bustled from worktop to stove. Chopping, stirring, tossing – but not in a rude way – as he roasted, boiled and sautéed his big fat fake-French heart out.

Didn't even look up from his pots as Roberta barged her way in. 'Hoy, *garçon*! When's dinner?'

That faux-Gallic accent was dialled up to full. 'Deener? DEENER? 'Ow am I supposed to create culinary miracles when your *stupide* police boy locks my freedge every time he goes on patrol? *C'est impossible!*'

She gave him a proper hard stare. 'Union Canal, remember?'

He backed away from the stove, wiping his shiny face on a tea towel, back to broad Brummie again. 'Giz a chance, eh? Albert only terned up with the main course five minutes ago.' Gérard pointed across the room with a ladle, towards the vast hairy carcass of a deer. Which not only wasn't already sizzling in a pan, the damn thing still had hooves, fur, and antlers on it.

'But I'm hungry *now*!'

'Youse can have it raw, if ye like – venison tartare wit' capers and shallots – but it'll be nicer if ye beggar off an' lerrus do me job.'

'But... But...'

He rolled his eyes. 'Hour, hour and a half, tops. Promise.'

'Gah...'

She spun on her heel and stomped away. Pushing past Sergeant Moore, who was just standing there, blocking the way like some sort of idiot Labrador.

Moore hurried after her. 'So, we've got time for a few more interviews, right?'

Bloody man was obsessed.

'Fine!' Roberta threw her hands in the air. 'If it'll stop you *wanging* on about it.' She stopped dead, turned, and poked him. 'But if I have to be nice to one more stuck-up, salt-of-the-earth-spouting tosspot, I'm going to explode.

No' figuratively: *literally*. BANG! Bits of Roberta all over the walls and ceiling.'

He was probably aiming for a cajoling smile, but it came off as patronising wankbaggery. 'Come on, I'm sure once we get going it won't be as bad as you—'

'BANG!' Another poke. 'And I'm taking *you* with me!'

'All right, all right: enough interviewing Tories for one day. How about we try some members of staff instead? That'll be better, won't it?'

Probably not.

Kinda hard to concentrate, when her innards were howling like a pack of wolves on a day-trip to the sausage factory, so Roberta didn't even bother. Just sat there and let Sergeant Moore ask all the questions.

Yes, you could argue that it was highly unprofessional to have a hungry sulk when you should be trying to catch a killer, but they already *had* a prime suspect. And besides, the hotel staff were all so *boring*: the gardener with the shaky hands and strong smell of 'medicinal cigarettes', who couldn't have held an opinion of his own if you'd duct-taped it to his hand; the cleaner with a thick Romanian accent, who spent most of the interview insisting she was in the country legally; and last, but by all means least, the spotty youth responsible for valet parking and washing all the guests' cars. And not one of the buggers had a single useful thing to say about Sir Reginald Bumfaced-Scumbag, Albert Nairn, or any sodding thing.

'Right, thank you for your time, Mr Hastings.' Moore put his notebook away and stood. 'Don't worry, we'll see ourselves out.' Not that it would've been difficult – the room was about the size of a phone box, plastered in posters of fast cars and ladies in very skimpy bikinis who for some reason seemed to have embarked on a career in automotive repair, only without any of the normal protective gear. Health and Safety would have a field day.

Hard to tell what the wee lad spent more time masturbating over – the cars or the women.

No wonder it smelled funky in here.

Bet a blacklight would make the sticky carpet shine like a radioactive Jackson Pollock.

'Detective Inspector? Hello?'

She blinked and there was Sergeant Moore, waving at her as if he'd been at it a while.

He grimaced. 'You still with us?'

Roberta pushed herself off the wall she'd been leaning against – because there was no way she was touching *any* of the furniture – and nodded. 'Right, keep up the good work, Mr...?'

'Hastings.' At least his voice had broken, that was something.

'Mr Hastings, right.' She followed Moore out of the room, stopping on the threshold to look back inside. Made eye contact with the spotty youth. 'Try to stop before you go blind, eh?' Then closed the door before he could do anything more than blush.

Roberta slouched along beside Sergeant Moore, not even bothering to cover her yawn. 'Well *that* was a waste of time.'

He rubbed his hands together, sounding pleased with himself. 'At least we're halfway through now. Twenty-three down, twenty-three to go.'

'Food.'

'We could probably knock a couple more off the list and—'

'Food! Food! Food! Food!'

He looked at her, sideways and troubled. 'Are you like this on every murder inquiry?'

Down the stairs at the end of the corridor.

'Murder inquiries are *nothing* like this. No one runs a Major Investigation Team with only three people, especially if one of them's an idiot who doesn't know wellington boots are a good idea when it's raining. You assemble a dirty-big squad full of experts and you delegate the living bejesus out of everything. Control it all from the centre of your web.' She pushed out through the door at the bottom of the stairs and into the lobby again. 'And that includes sending someone out for bacon butties, cups of tea, and anything else that takes your fancy.' Marching across the tartan carpet towards the dining room. 'What you *don't* do is struggle on all day with an empty stomach, personally interviewing three-dozen stuck-up buggers, when you could be squirrelled away in a posh hotel room playing Hide-the-Nutella with your wife!'

The dining room was laid out for a full service: all the tables set with white cloths, napkins, silverware, and more glasses than anyone could possibly need during the course of one meal.

Roberta marched past the lot of them and banged into the kitchen. 'Well?'

Gérard turned a dimpled smile on her, his rosy cheeks all round and sweaty in the steamy kitchen as he struck a pose: feet together, back straight, one finger pointing at the ceiling tiles. 'Ze great Gérard de Larosière 'as done eet again! I geeve to you ze culinary masterpiece.' He turned to make a sweeping gesture towards an array of pots, pans, and dishes. 'Wash your 'ands and prepare for ze experience of a lifetime. *Alléz vite!*'

'All right.' She narrowed her eyes at him. 'But this better be worth it, or I'm coming back in here and stuffing you like a Christmas turkey. With your own head.'

The view from the dining room was probably quite impressive, when it wasn't dinging down at nine o'clock on a Saturday night. The rain rendered everything in depressing shades of greeny-grey, and even though the sun wasn't supposed to set for another hour and a bit, it was already getting dark out there. Well, even darker.

Susan polished off the last of her soup and smiled across the table. 'Wasn't that lovely?' She was all done up in a nice floral frock, with heels and a matching bag. Unlike Roberta, in her 'ASK ME ABOUT MY RADICAL LESBIAN FEMINIST AGENDA' T-shirt and tumbled jeans.

Could probably fit fifty people in here, but the room was deserted except for the two of them, dining by candlelight. A nice bottle of Chenin Blanc chilling in an ice bucket at the side of the table.

'A toast!' Susan raised her glass. 'To romantic getaways.'

Roberta clinked glasses with her, then had a glug of lovely cold wine. 'Aye, romantic for *you*, maybe. Some of us've been interrogating Tory tosspots and getting soaked all day.' But she kept a smile on her face as she spoke, so *technically* it didn't count as a whinge.

'Well, *I* think it's lovely.' Susan reached across the table and took Roberta's hand, looking up at her through her eyelashes. 'Maybe after this we should—'

The door to the kitchen thumped open and in barged the wee weird ginger woman, pushing a hostess-trolley kind of thing. 'All done?' Cheery smile and cheery voice – no doubt still in a heightened erogenous state after that flash of Old Faithful. She gathered up their empty bowls. 'How was your velouté de navet, with a parmesan tuile and smoked truffle-oil emulsion?'

'You're no' fooling anyone. Neep soup's neep soup, no matter how you dress it up.'

'Robbie!' Susan turned a beam in the woman's direction. 'It was lovely, Janey, thank you. Who knew turnips could be so scrumptious?'

'Excellent.' Wee Weird Janey clinked their empty bowls down on top of the trolley and came back with two plates, placing one in front of each of them with a theatrical flourish. 'Here we have venison carpaccio *avec mousse de navet et sorbet aux racines.*' Kissing her fingertips as a grand finale. 'Enjoy.' She backed away from the table, taking her trolley and her weirdness through to the kitchen again.

Susan speared a wafer-thin slice of dark purple meat and popped it into her mouth. Chewing with her eyes closed. 'Delicious!'

Roberta pushed the cold-looking lump of orange stuff about her plate. Whatever it was, it looked extremely dodgy. 'How well do you know the rest of the guests?'

'Well, Mortimer's the firm's senior partner, so he's all right, and you've met Agatha. Adriana's a good assistant – very thorough when she gets her teeth into something.' A shrug made Susan's cleavage do very naughty things. 'The rest are a mixture of clients and strangers. I'd know them to talk to, but that's it.'

Quick look left and right to make sure no one had sneaked into the dining room when they weren't looking. 'What about Sir Reginald Wibbly-Whatnot?'

'Robbie! The poor man's *dead.*'

'Aye, aye, boo hoo, stop the clocks and cover the budgie,

etcetera. What about his shady dealings? Your firm involved in any of that?'

Susan went in for another slice of venison. 'Well, *Mortimer* mostly deals with Sir Reginald's business affairs and I'm sure they're not in the least bit shady, thank you very much.'

OK, nothing else for it, Roberta was going to have to try the slippery orange whatever-it-was. It slithered away from her fork, but she finally managed to dig out a chunk and stuck it in her gob. Strangely cold and sweet and earthy, all at the same time. 'What makes you think they're no' shady? There's sod-all...' Why did the whatever-it-was taste familiar, but wrong at the same time? 'Is this *carrot* ice cream?'

'*Sorbet aux racines*. Eat up.'

Roberta stared at the closed kitchen door. 'What kind of sick weirdo makes *carrot* ice cream?'

'And for your information: I know Sir Reginald's business dealings aren't "dodgy", because our firm wouldn't be handling them if they were. Beresford, Ackroyd, and Edgware is *very* highly respected in corporate law circles.'

She shook her head. 'Carrot ice cream.' Then tried a wee bit more. Actually, it wasn't so bad once you got used to the idea.

Susan scooted her chair forward, dropping her voice to a whisper. 'If you ask me, it's Lord Fitzroy-Galbraith you should be looking at. I hear he wanted to develop a planned village on the estate – high-end villas and holiday homes. You'd make a killing from the London get-away-for-the-weekend set.'

'This turnip mousse is OK too.'

Maybe Gérard de Larosière wasn't as daft as he looked?

Susan's eyes widened. 'I hear Sir Reginald had the deciding vote on the planning authority. What if he said no, and Lord Fitzroy-Galbraith *killed* him?'

Roberta sat back and smiled at her. 'Aye, all right, Miss

Marple. You leave the detecting to the professionals or I'll have to ask you to assist me with my inquiries.' Topping that one off with an extremely dirty wink, sending Susan into blushing giggles.

Susan stood and leaned across the table for a kiss. 'You'll never take me alive, copper.'

Roberta levered herself out of her seat and was *just* about to join her when the kitchen door banged open and Weird Janey poked her head into the dining room again.

'Who's ready for their main course?'

Some people's timing was utter bollocks.

Roberta kissed Susan on the forehead – just a wee peck, not enough to wake her – and slipped from the room.

The corridor outside 'Laphroaig' was dark as a lawyer's soul. Not *Susan's* soul, obviously: she was the exception that proved the rule. But the rest of them could fester in the gloomy heat of Satan's bumhole for all eternity and it still wouldn't be long enough.

'Let there be light.' But when she flicked the switch in the hallway, nothing happened. So, just to be on the safe side, Roberta clicked it up and down a half dozen more times.

Still nothing.

OK...

She pulled out her mobile and called up the torch app. Swinging the thin cold beam across the corridor, where it glittered back from the long-dead eyes of stuffed animals. OK, that was more than a little unnerving.

Turning her back on them, she followed the phone's torchlight to the end of the corridor, freezing just inside the doors. Listening.

Voices, muffled in the darkness, wafted through from the other side. Low and conspiratorial.

Roberta put her hand on the door and pushed through into the gloom beyond.

15

It wasn't *quite* as dark on the balcony that ran along this side of the lobby. A wan grey-ish light filtered in through the windows, thickening the shadows to solid black. But down below, on the lobby floor, two circles of light had converged in front of the huge metal stag.

Roberta switched her phone's torch off and crept forwards, ears straining.

'*...did he?*'

'*Oh, like you wouldn't believe!*'

Not quite whispering, but not far off it.

She edged her way to the staircase and padded down it on soft careful feet, not making a sound.

'*Then I don't suppose we've got any choice, do we?*'

'*Nope.*'

Closer, skirting the back end of the statue like a ninja.

Closer. Closer.

'*Still, at least—*'

Roberta leapt from the shadows. 'What-ho, sharny bumholes?'

Swear to God, the pair of them leapt about six foot in the air and screamed like frightened rabbits.

She grinned as PC McKinnon and Sergeant Moore tried to get their breath back, hands clutching their chests, faces going from pale-as-a-sheet to beetroot.

'Bloody hell.' Moore stared at her. 'Frightened the *life* out of me!'

McKinnon nodded. Trying to pretend he hadn't just pooped himself. 'Ma'am.'

Well, he wasn't getting off that lightly.

She poked him in the chest. 'I've got one word to say to you, Constable: wellington sodding boots!'

A puzzled chin-in frown. 'But that's *three* words.'

'So's "rectal shoe insertion". Which is what you deserve for letting me tromp through the bastarding monsoon this morning when there were wellington boots in the Land Rover!'

'Ah... Erm, here:' he dug into one of the pockets on his stabproof and produced a blue plastic torch. Clicked the button and handed it over. 'Found them in a utility cupboard. Got one for the Sarge too.'

As peace offerings went, it wasn't great, but never look a gift torch in the mouth.

She tried it out on the cavernous lobby. The beam wasn't exactly lighthouse-bright. Better than her phone, though. 'What happened to the proper lights?'

'They switched off the generator at ten to save on diesel. Everyone's meant to be asleep anyway...'

Sergeant Moore leaned back against the statue's plinth. Arms crossed. 'I *still* say we should lock them in their rooms. Stop them getting out and up to things.'

'Aye, but what if there's a fire, Sarge? Health and Safety would do their nit if we got everyone killed.'

Moore stared at him. '"Nut", you twit. Do their *nut*.'

'What did I say?'

'You said "do their nit."'

'Did I? That's—'

'Oh, for God's sake. Shut up, the pair of you.' Roberta shone her torch in their eyes to drive the point home. 'We're no' locking people in their rooms. The wee loon might be a nutwit, but he's right. Here's the deal: we split the night into three shifts. I'll take first go; McKinnon, you're midnight till four; and Sergeant Moore can do the dawn patrol.'

McKinnon checked his watch, face like a spanked puppy. 'But it's gone half ten now! How come I've got a four-hour shift and you've only got ninety minutes?'

'Cos I'm in charge, and nobody likes a whinge.' She gave him a poke. 'And don't just find yourself somewhere cosy to hole up: *patrol*. Make sure all the doors and windows are locked too.'

Sergeant Moore jerked his chin towards the front of the hotel. 'What about Albert Nairn? He's got keys, remember?'

'Aye, but he'll no' risk anything if he knows we're waiting for him. So make sure you swing your torches about a bit – make a real *show* out of being on guard. OK?'

'OK.' McKinnon put his hand in the middle, palm down, and, after a pause, Moore put his hand on top of it.

They both looked at her, eyebrows up, waiting for that third hand on the pile.

'What are you, six?' She shooed them away. 'Go on: sod off the pair of you and get some rest.' Pointing a finger at McKinnon. 'I'll see *you* at twelve.'

Somewhere off in the depths of the hotel, a grandfather clock chimed eleven long sonorous bongs as Roberta wandered along the corridor, playing her new torch across the stuffed animals and oil paintings.

Who thought it was a good idea to fill what was obviously meant to be a luxury hotel with dead things? Place was like a furry mausoleum.

She tried the window at the end of the corridor. Locked.

Then turned and headed back the way she'd come, past all those stiff limbs and wings and claws and beaks.

Every now and then, there'd be this strange noise, like distant voices, but by the time she'd got there, the room or passageway was empty. Not voices at all, just the sounds of an ancient house feeling its age.

Roberta stepped out into the lobby again.

Or maybe it was ghosts?

Christ knew there were enough dead badgers and crows and foxes and deer in here to haunt the place. Call in Ghostbusters and they'd get trampled in the stampede.

With any luck, the long-dead menagerie would find Lord Fitzroy-Galbraith wandering the halls on his tod one night and gore the misogynistic bugger to death. Then eat him.

She tried the hotel's front doors again – locked – turned around and headed through to the library, shoulders drooping, feet scuffing on the tartan carpet. Big room, double height. Each of its four walls were clarted with books, their spines glittering in the yellowy torchlight, all segregated into genres and formats – the crime fiction paperbacks banished to the furthest reaches of the upstairs balcony, going by the garish spines and lurid titles. Lots of polished wood and dead things in display cabinets. Windows looking out onto the rainy gloom. A fireplace large enough to roast a whole lawyer in.

Pfff...

God this was boring.

Roberta checked her watch, but it was still only 23:08. Nearly *an hour* to go.

Going to be a *long* night.

Come on, come on, come on...

She stood in the corridor right outside 'GLENKEITH', watching the numbers tick down. Nine, eight, seven, six, five, four, three, two, one ... that grandfather clock whirred into life again, sounding its long echoing bongs.

And, at long last, the witching hour had arrived.

Roberta raised her fist to knock, but before her knuckles could get anywhere near the door, it opened and PC McKinnon slithered his way out into the corridor, easing the door shut behind him. He had his police boots in his hand, a big toe performing a cheeky peekaboo through his left sock. Dressed in the full Police Scotland ninja black. His voice was barely a whisper. 'Barbara's sleeping.'

'Oh aye? All shagged out is she? You dirty sod.' Roberta tapped him on the stabproof chest with her torch, causing angular shadows to dance across his sticky-out Adam's apple. 'Just make sure nothing happens on your watch, OK? After last night, I need all the shuteye I can get.'

She turned and swaggered off, humming 'Patricia the Stripper', leaving the hotel in McKinnon's semi-capable hands.

No, Mr Horse, you can't come into the car. Because you're too hairy and you smell of cheese. No. Don't get into the car, can't you see it's on fire? Stop knocking on the roof with your horrible hooves, you can't come into the burning—

Roberta spluttered upright in bed with an ear-thrummeling snork and sat there, in the dark, blinking at... Where the hell was she? This wasn't home.

She rubbed a hand across her face and peered out into the darkness.

Phone. Phone on the bedside cabinet.

Picking it up set the screen glowing, banishing a little bit of the gloom, revealing a tartan bedspread, with murderous threats of further tartan beyond. Ah. Right. Skirivour Castle Hotel. The poncy palace of plaid.

She sagged back into her pillows and let free a jaw-popping yawn. Threw in a little burp for luck. Sighed.

Time was it?

The glowing red numbers on her phone read, '02:16'.

Gah...

Far too early for crap like—

Was that voices?

She sat up again as a faint thump sounded somewhere out in the hall.

OK, there was definitely somebody there.

Roberta scrambled from the bed and into her T-shirt and jeans – no time to waste pulling on underwear, this was strictly a commando exercise. Grabbed the torch on her way from the room. Locking the door behind her. Just in case.

Dear Lord, it was dark.

The torch's beam slid across the tartan carpet and up across the walls. No sign of anything but the creepy stuffed animals in their creepy display cases.

She crept her way down the corridor and eased the door at the end open, stepping out onto the balcony. Stupid torch wasn't nearly as bright as it'd been when McKinnon handed it over – the light a bit yellow and feeble. And getting more feeble with every minute.

'Oh, for God's sake...'

Trust that wee idiot to give her the dud.

Bashing it against her palm a few times made it brighten a little, but not much. Still, better than nothing. She played it across the lobby to the opposite balcony. Nobody there.

Nobody down at ground level either. Well, unless they were hiding behind the monster stag.

Roberta picked her way down the stairs and out onto the lobby floor. Checked around the back of the statue, just in case.

No one.

She tried a sort of shouty whisper. 'McKinnon?'

No reply.

The front-door handles wouldn't turn when she tried them, so they were still locked – the key sticking out of its keyhole. Not the most robust of home-security measures, but it should stop Albert Nairn getting his key in the other side.

Right. So it was time to play 'Find The Useless Constable'.

Left or right?

Six of one.

She went left, following the circle of torchlight along the horrible plaid carpet, down the corridor. You'd think they'd get tired of taxidermy and tartan, wouldn't you? Most of the dead animals weren't even that realistic. Yeah, they were *real*, but somehow the stuffing had rendered them like badly drawn caricatures. The poses stiff enough to make it look as if they'd never been alive in the first place. Like there was more chance of bumping into one of Nairn's monstrosities out on the hills than one of these poor frozen things.

Roberta followed the corridor around the corner, only to find some sort of horror shining a torch right in her eyes.

'Gah!'

She danced backwards until the wall stopped her going any further, grabbed a pheasant in its bell jar from the nearest sideboard and hefted it over her head as a weapon...

The monster did exactly the same thing, at exactly the same time.

Oh you silly *sod*.

Roberta lowered the pheasant and the Roberta in the oversized gilt-edged mirror did the same. Well, it was an easy mistake to make: creepy castle in the middle of creepy nowhere, surrounded by creepy things, hunting for a creepy killer. Was bound to put you a bit on edge.

She scowled at her traitorous reflection, with its rumpled face and hair that looked like an accident in a black-and-white candyfloss factory. Still, on the bright side, if her appearance startled *her*, it would probably scare the living crap out of anyone else.

The pheasant went back where she'd found it and Roberta stepped through into the conservatory.

Silence.

She stared up at the glass roof – completely clear. It had *actually* stopped raining. Not only that, a fissure opened in the thick cloud cover, growing as she stood there, flooding the conservatory with soft grey moonlight.

Couches and armchairs were arranged in little groups, orbiting wicker coffee tables – their glass tops glistening as she drifted her torch across them. Another shock-horror: the place wasn't littered with furry corpses. As if they'd finally run out of dead things to put on display.

She crept around the conservatory, peering behind every couch to make sure no sneaky wee gamekeeper-slash-murderer was hiding there. Which they weren't. Then checked the French doors out to the garden were locked.

The handle twisted beneath her fingertips and both doors swung open on silent hinges.

That wasn't good: they'd been locked the last time she'd checked, at the end of her shift – just before the idiot McKinnon took over.

Outside, moonbeams caught the mist rising from the dark world, making it glow like it was haunted. That gap in the clouds widened even further, bathing the gardens in cold dead light...

Cheery thought.

She had another bash at whispershouting, 'McKinnon? Where the hell are you, you useless wee sheep-shagger?' Silence. 'McKinnon?'

So what was she supposed to do now? Close the doors and lock them, potentially shutting the idiot outside, or leave them open and risk Albert Nairn getting in?

She turned and frowned back into the hotel.

Assuming Nairn wasn't *already* inside, and this was his escape route. In which case locking the doors and pocketing the key might trap him inside. Where they could catch the sinister bastard. But knowing her luck, it would just end up with PC McKinnon hammering on the windows at four in the morning, demanding to be let in before the pixies, or that horned squirrel-thing got him.

Ah well, it was his own silly fault.

She pulled the French doors closed, locked them both, and pocketed the key. Curled her free hand into a fist. Then turned and marched back into the main body of the hotel.

If Albert Nairn really *had* snuck in, he was in for a nasty surprise.

They'd cleared away the tables and chairs from the wedding, leaving the ballroom empty and hollow. No Albert Nairn.

He wasn't in the billiard room either, where the only sound was the grandfather clock, ticking in the corner.

Nor in the dining room. Kitchen. Lobby...

Roberta stepped into the library, running her torch over the chairs and bookshelves. Moonlight spilled through the windows, painting the tartan carpet in colour-stealing shades of grey.

Beginning to look like PC McKinnon had locked himself outside. OK, so *technically* she'd done the locking, but that's what he got for mucking about when he should've been patrolling the hotel. Not her fault he was an idiot.

Still, better go back to the conservatory and let him in again. Give him one of her famous motivational speeches about doing what you're bloody well told. And maybe a free kick up the arse as well.

She turned back towards the door and froze.

Bugger…

There was a body, lying face down by the science fiction novels, in full Police Scotland kit, partially hidden behind an antique leather sofa. PC McKinnon.

Roberta hurried over, felt for a pulse.

Nothing.

Damn it!

She hauled him over onto his back. Was he breathing?

How could he be breathing if he didn't have a pulse.

Yeah, but finding a pulse was notoriously difficult, wasn't it?

Only one way to check for sure.

She hauled back a hand and gave him a good hard slap.

'Aaargh!' McKinnon sat up, hands windmilling, like a small child trapped in a tumble drier. Eyes wide and darting around. Slapped cheek already going red in the torchlight. 'Where…?'

Roberta pulled her hand back for a second go. 'If you've just been having a kip, God help you.'

'Whhh…' One side of his face scrunched up. 'Ow!' Then he reached for the back of his head, fingertips probing at the ginger hair.

She hauled him forward and shone her torch there – blood. Not a heap of it, but enough. It dotted the crown of a proper egg-shaped lump that hadn't been there before. 'What the hell happened?'

'Someone thumped me.' God, with a razor-sharp mind like that, it was a wonder McKinnon hadn't been promoted to DI yet.

She helped him struggle to his feet. 'It's OK, you're...'

A noise out in the corridor made her spin around.

Someone was lurking in the darkened lobby, but before her torch beam found them, they were off, running.

Nairn!

She let go of McKinnon and he promptly collapsed on the floor again as she leapt for the library doors. 'COME BACK HERE!'

Out into the lobby, making for the main entrance.

Moonbeams spilled in through the windows, painting cold white bars across the echoing space, making the dark darker.

A flash of grey and the bugger she was chasing leapt across a patch of light – definitely Nairn. Couldn't see his face, but he was still wearing that spooky pelt-cloak thing, with horns on the hood.

'YOU CAN'T GET AWAY, NAIRN!'

He skidded to a halt at the front doors and rattled them.

Locked.

Ya wee beauty!

Then he turned the key and shouldered them open, bursting out into the night.

Sod.

16

Roberta sprinted past that stupid metal stag and barrelled through the open doors.

Outside, the moon's glow cast everything in black and white, carpeting the wet grass with a billion tiny stars, turning the woods on the other side of the hotel gardens into a wall of silhouettes.

Her bare feet ploughed into the cold hard gravel.

'Ow, ow, ow, ow!'

It was like some sadist had carpeted the world with blocks of Lego.

'Ow, ow, ow, ow...' and then her toes squelched onto the wet grass. Bliss.

Nairn disappeared around the corner and she hammered after him, squishing and slipping on the waterlogged turf, down the side of the building.

He was fast. Faster than her, anyway, arms and legs pumping. Probably helped that he had shoes on. But the gap between them was widening as he took a hard left, cutting across the moonlit gardens, making for the coal-black treeline.

'COME BACK HERE, YOU CREEPY WEE SHITE!'

He didn't, though, because no bugger ever did.

Nairn was getting away...

Then that gap in the clouds closed up, swallowing the moon whole and plunging the world into darkness again.

She whipped her torch up, the beam *just* bright enough to catch the back of Nairn's roadkill cloak. Even further away now.

Argh...

Roberta leaned into it, huffing and puffing – closing the gap a little ... and then Nairn vanished into the woods.

Oh God, it'd been bad enough trying to follow him last time, and that was in daylight. Now? In the dark, at night, when he was very probably armed? Yeah, this maybe wasn't the best idea she'd ever had. But what was she supposed to do, *let* him get away?

And then her torch did its stupid cutting-out trick again.

She skip-hop-slithered to a stop and whacked the thing against her palm. 'Come on, you piece of crap...'

It gave one last sulk of dim yellow light and died. Didn't matter how many times she battered the wee bugger, it didn't come on again. Dead.

Well, that kinda put the arsehole on chasing Albert Nairn into the woods, didn't it?

Still, it wasn't as if he could actually *go* anywhere.

She hauled in a deep breath. 'I KNOW WHERE YOU LIVE!'

Then bent double, grabbed her knees, and wheezed for a bit. Been far too much running about, this holiday. In fact, if she was being brutally honest, this whole trip had been a bit of a wankfest.

Puffing out a heavy breath, Roberta straightened up.

Just have to head out mob-handed in the morning to House-of-Horrors Cottage and arrest Nairn. Three of them, one of him. Should be doable.

After all, what's the worst that could happen?

As if on cue, a distant rumble of thunder sounded in the mountains, and the rain rushed in on its wake, battering into her, drenching her right through on the way back to the hotel.

'I sodding *hate* weddings.'

The tartan carpet darkened around Roberta's bare feet as she hammered on the door marked, 'THE BALVENIE'. Hair plastered to her head, T-shirt sticking in all the wrong places, jeans being overly familiar with her underwear-free parts, as she dripped. 'SERGEANT MOORE, OPEN UP!'

The door cracked open and there was Moore, in his Spider-Man pyjamas, yawning and blinking. 'Time is it?' He screwed up one eye and peered at his watch. Sagged. 'Not my shift till *four*.' Then gave her a peer too. 'Why are you all wet?'

'Nairn.' She ran a hand through her hair and flicked the water against the walls. 'He snuck in and bashed McKinnon over the back of the head.'

'Son of a bitch.' Wiping the sleep from his eyes. 'What do you need me to do? Is Mikey OK?'

'Boy's got a head like a curling stone.' She turned and stomped back down the corridor. 'Wake the buggers up, every last one of them. We need to make sure Nairn's no' crucified anyone else.'

Roberta wrapped another three-or-four foot of bandages around PC McKinnon's ginger napper. 'Will you hold still?'

The wee lad was still a bit wobbly, but at least his colour had returned. Possibly due to the very large brandy she'd liberated from the hotel bar and made him drink.

The open library door gave a clear view down into the lobby, where Sergeant Moore herded every single guest and staff member down the hotel stairs by torchlight. The whole lot shuffling about in their PJs, hair all squint, eyes all puffy, yawning and scratching. Whinging about what time do you call this and there better be an emergency and you had better believe the Chief Constable was a *close* personal friend who would *not* be pleased.

Roberta tied the bandage off, nice and tight.

'OW!'

'Don't be such a wimp.'

Outside, in the lobby, Moore held up a hand. 'I know you're all tired, but let's everyone just pay attention and we'll get you back to your beds as soon as possible.' He consulted a clipboard. 'Mr and Mrs Reeves?'

The fusty man stepped forwards, dragging his wife with him. The pair of them done up in matching floral jim-jams. 'I wish to make a *strongly* worded complaint to your superior officer!'

'Good for you. Now, off to bed.' Moore ticked something on his clipboard. 'Mr and Mrs Beresford?'

'Present.'

'Thank you. Off to bed for you too.'

Roberta double-checked her knot. 'You didn't see *anything*?'

The constable shrugged. 'One minute I was checking the library windows and then: *pow*.' He rubbed his cheek. 'Next thing I know, you're belting me one.'

'It was Nairn. I chased him off into the woods. At great personal risk, I might add.' She sat back and examined her handiwork. 'You'll live.' Mind you, there was *one* thing bugging her. 'When was it? When did he attack you?'

McKinnon frown-winced. 'Half one? No, tell a lie, cos

I heard the grandfather clock in the billiard room striking quarter to two just before I came in here.'

Quarter to two, and she got up at what, quarter past-ish? Which meant Albert Nairn was sneaking about the hotel for at least half an hour, completely unsupervised.

She wandered over to the library window and scowled into the rainy darkness. Nairn was out there, somewhere, probably bunkering down in that taxidermy mausoleum of his, getting ready for a siege. But for thirty minutes he'd had the run of Skirivour Castle Hotel while everyone else was unconscious.

'What the hell were you up to, you animal-stuffing little freak?'

With everyone sent back to bed, the lobby had returned to its gloomy quiet, but only Sergeant Moore, PC McKinnon, and Roberta were there to enjoy it.

Roberta leaned back against the stag's plinth and took a sook on her e-cigarette. Blew a cloud of strawberry steam at the ceiling. 'Well?'

'All present and correct.' Moore held up his clipboard, showing off all the scored-out names. 'Whatever Albert Nairn was up to, it wasn't killing anyone.'

McKinnon prodded at his bandaged head again. 'Well, at least that's something, right? Right?'

'Aye, that or we got in the way before he could do it.' She sent another strawberry cloud skyward. 'Get your arse off to bed: Sergeant Moore will take the rest of your watch. But first thing tomorrow: we're going to hunt Albert Buggering Nairn down and arrest his murdering arse.'

'Yes, ma'am.' The wee loon scampered off, leaving them alone in the lobby.

Roberta gave Moore a good once-over. Scruffy hair, rabbit-skin slippers, red-and-blue webby pyjamas. 'What is it with you and Spider-Man?'

'Everyone's got to have a hobby.'

He and McKinnon were as bad as each other. Mad as a tea party.

She shook her head and left him to it.

17

The relentless hiss of rain slithered in through the open hotel doors. Dawn hadn't so much broken as cracked, letting only the thinnest hint of daylight slip across the drowning world.

Standing on the nasty tartan threshold, Roberta pulled the zip up on her still-damp high-vis jacket, then did a little pirouette with her arms out in true catwalk fashion. 'What every well-dressed sexy police officer is wearing this season.'

Susan smiled, stepped in close, licked her own thumb, and scrubbed at something on Roberta's chin. 'Honestly, you've got breakfast all over you.'

'I'm a passionate person.'

'And don't I know it.' She wrapped her arms around Roberta and gave her a long wriggly kiss that tasted faintly of sausage, bacon, two fried eggs, baked beans, and a slice of haggis.

Mmm, sexy Sunday breakfast.

By the time they parted lips, Sergeant Moore was staring off into the corner, face a hot shade of Barbie pink.

Susan straightened the lapels of the high-vis. 'Are you *sure* you're going to be OK?'

'Well, just in case...' Roberta dipped a hand into a jacket pocket and pulled out the little stuffed mouse. 'You look after Teeny Roberta for me till I get back, OK?'

'What...?' She looked at it, in its little trousers, bra, and socks with what could only be described as a mixture of revulsion and horror. Holding it between two fingertips, like it was a little plastic bag full of soft, warm dog poo. 'What the hell is *this* revolting thing?'

'Now, if Albert Nairn kills us all, you'll have something to remember me by.'

Susan held it out at arm's length. 'Robbie, when people give their loved one something to look after till their return, it's meant to be something *romantic*. A family heirloom. Jewellery. Not a dead mouse!'

'Look, she's even wearing a tiny Old Faithful.'

'Urgh…' Chin in, mouth curdling.

Sergeant Moore did one of those loud on-purpose, *'ahem'*s, making a whole pantomime of checking his watch. 'That's PC McKinnon back now, so we'd better get going.' He tipped a nod at Susan. 'Thanks for holding down the fort for us.'

'Not a problem, I'll make sure everyone stays in their rooms.'

God help anyone that stepped out of line, she could be right nippy with a righteous wind behind her.

'Aye, and if they give you any trouble?' Roberta pointed at the stuffed animal dangling from her fingers. 'Set Mini-Me-Mouse on them.' Then turned and marched out to join Moore and PC McKinnon beneath the portico.

The rain was every bit as bad as yesterday, lumping it down from a blackened sky. Bouncing off the sodden ground and shattering the surface of what used to be puddles but were now auditioning as lochs.

Being the lowest on the Police Scotland totem pole, McKinnon didn't get one of the two high-vis waterproofs, instead he had to make do with a dull-grey outdoor jacket of his own, with his stabproof vest and fluorescent-yellow waistcoat on over the top. Peaked cap sitting a bit squint due to the messy wodge of bandages wrapped around his head. The lad was almost buried under the massive pile of stuff in his arms. 'Little help!'

Sergeant Moore extracted a couple of the heavier items. 'You get everything?'

'Binoculars from the Landy; every bit of MOE and protective gear I could find; and the first-aid kit, just in case Albert Nairn shoots and doesn't kill one-slash-all of us.'

'Fair doos.' Moore handed the hooly bar to Roberta and followed it up with a riot helmet.

The three-foot metal rod felt violently familiar in her hands – an oversized crowbar's claw at one end, a spike and a wedge at the other. Was there *anything* more fun than whacking someone's front window in with one of these, or cracking the door off their secret-stash cupboard? Or just going crazy apeshite on the bonnet of their car with the spikey bit? ... Well, anything that didn't require taking most of your clothes off?

Her new riot helmet was a bit snug, and brought with it the unmistakable whiff of sheep, but hey-ho.

While she was giving the hooly bar a couple of experimental swings, Moore struggled his way into a set of Method Of Entry gear – gloves, elbow and wrist protectors, knee and shin guards. They looked ridiculous on over his jeans and high-vis.

'And last but not least.' PC McKinnon held out a pair of wellington boots. 'I saw these and thought of you.'

'You wee dancer.' Roberta plonked her bum down on the top step, pulled off her trainers, and hauled the wellies on. About two sizes bigger than her feet, but at least they'd keep her socks dry. Even if they did shauchle about a bit.

Susan stepped out onto the gravel, clutching a trio of brollies. 'Don't forget your umbrellas.' Not letting go when she handed one to Roberta. 'And don't take any silly risks!'

'What, like this?' Roberta grabbed a handful of Susan's

bum and gave her a damn good snogging, with extra tongues as Moore and McKinnon shuffled their feet and looked anywhere other than here.

Sergeant Moore did his throat-clearing thing again. 'Can we go now? Or do you two want to get a room?'

The forest track squelched beneath her feet; wellington boots making wub-wonk noises as they flapped about. Should've worn her trainers. OK, so her feet would be drowned puddings by now, but see if she needed to run away from a gun-totin' redneck taxidermist? These bloody wellies would be the death of her.

Wub-wonk, wub-wonk, wub-wonk...

Up at the front of their little high-vis expedition, Moore checked Gérard/Tony's hand-drawn map from yesterday. Nodding as if he could tell the difference between one soggy tree and another soggy tree in this massive collection of soggy bloody trees, as they slogged through the rain-drenched gloom of a Scottish summer.

But, on the bright side: at least this pishy weather was keeping the midges at home.

From the tail end of their caterpillar, PC McKinnon sniffed and shuffled – keeping his voice low. 'What do we do if Nairn won't come quietly?'

'Course he'll come quietly.' *Wub-wonk, wub-wonk, wub-wonk...*

'But he's got a gun! Nothing we've got will stop a bullet. Or a shotgun cartridge. We've not even done a risk assessment!'

'Aye, we did. While you were off getting the stuff, Sergeant Moore and me did one, didn't we, Sergeant Moore?'

Moore glanced back at them, a row of creases between his eyebrows. 'Not really.' He looked over her head at McKinnon.

'We decided that if Albert Nairn comes at us with a gun: we throw you at him and run away.'

The constable's eyes bulged. 'That's not—'

'He won't come out shooting.' *Wub-wonk, wub-wonk, wub-wonk...* 'It's the Scottish Highlands, no' Bonny and Clydeside. We'll talk to him, he'll come quietly, we'll cuff him and take him back to the hotel for a bit of being-locked-in-a-room-till-Inverness-gets-here. End of.'

'Aye, but what if he—'

'First sign of him kicking off, we go back to the hotel and wait him out. No taking risks, no buggering about. There, you happy now?'

McKinnon curled his top lip and kept on shuffling. Looking like he was about to pee himself. 'Kinda...?'

Roberta shook her head at Sergeant Moore. 'They always grow PCs this wet up here?'

Moore grimaced back at her. 'Just try not to get us all killed, OK?'

She gave him a grin. 'Do my best, but I'm not promising anything.'

Roberta hunkered down and peered over the same knot of brambles they'd hidden behind yesterday. The bone-riddled clearing that surrounded Albert Nairn's personal haunted-house-of-creepiness was every bit as uninviting as last time. Only wetter.

PC McKinnon's eyes widened as he took it all in. 'Good God... It's like something out of a *horror* movie.' Never let it be said the boy didn't pay attention.

Sergeant Moore flexed his hands in his MOE gloves. 'So, do we split up, or stick together?'

'Easier target if we stick together, Sarge. Split up and we can surround the place.'

Roberta thumped him one. 'No one's splitting up till we see what's what.' She stuck out her hand. 'Give us the binoculars.'

McKinnon handed them over and she had a good squint at the cottage.

Didn't look any less spooky in close-up. Could see the little parade of dead things lined up along the inside of the windowsills, the drawn curtains acting as a backdrop for their Passion Play. And that wasn't a euphemism, either – it was a bunch of stuffed mice re-enacting the crucifixion with a stoat Jesus. Which had to be an instant Go-Straight-To-Hell card. The curtains on the left-hand side of the door were closed too. An empty bottle of Grouse sat on the porch, next to the rocking chair.

That would be Albert Nairn – sitting there last night, plotting his revenge, drinking up his nerve to storm the hotel and murder some other poor bugger. Not that Sir Reginald Bradbury-Scott counted as a poor bugger…

PC McKinnon tapped her on the shoulder. 'What if he's gone out?'

'In this weather?'

'Could be hunting.'

She swept the binoculars across the front of the property again. 'Then we can sneak inside and surprise him when he gets home, can't we?'

'Oh. Right. OK…'

Sergeant Moore hunkered down beside her. 'You see anything?'

'No smoke coming from the chimney. Curtains are drawn… Might be having a long lie? Looks like he's necked a bottle of Grouse, so it could be Hangover-From-Hell time.'

'Or Mikey's right and he's out.'

She handed the binoculars back. 'One way to find out.'

At least there'd been no sign of a rifle barrel poking out through a gap in the curtains, ready to pick off any sexy former detective chief inspectors in their borrowed high-vis jackets.

Deep breath, and Roberta stepped out from behind the brambles – rain patter-clicking off her shoulders and riot helmet as she picked her way up the path, keeping her eyes on the woodchip-and-gravel, high-stepping over a couple of fishing-line tripwires. After all, just because the one Sergeant Moore set off yesterday made nothing more deadly than a noise, it didn't mean Nairn hadn't hooked one of them up to a bunch of shotgun shells wrapped in roofing nails...

Which was a comforting thought.

And something she really should have considered *before* leaving the safety of the bushes.

Could've sent McKinnon if there were going to be IEDs.

The wooden porch creaked beneath her wellington boots. Safe at last.

When she turned, there was Sergeant Moore and his halfwit sidekick, tiptoeing their way after her. Doing the same elaborate footwork to get past Nairn's tripwires, like a cut-price Laurel and Hardy.

She snapped on a pair of blue nitrile gloves and tried the door handle... It turned, nice and easy. Not locked. A gentle push sent it swinging open with a warm sonorous groan.

Oh crap.

She stared in through the open door.

They were too late.

Dead animals still littered the shelves, but Albert Nairn had joined those hanging from the rafters. The rope around his neck went up and around one of the exposed beams, a kitchen chair lying on its side by his feet as he swayed in the draught from the open door.

Roberta shook her head. 'You silly, *silly* sod.'

A voice behind her: *'What?'* Then Sergeant Moore crept onto the porch and peered over her shoulder, into the cottage. 'Oh…'

She stepped across the threshold, looking up into that slack face. Eyes part open, the tip of his pale tongue just visible between his lips.

'Looks like he left a note.' Moore picked up a sheet of yellowed paper from the kitchen table, reading out loud. '"To whom it may concern. I have decided to take my own life, rather than live like a caged animal in one of your gaols." Spelled the old-fashioned way. "I hereby confess to the killing of Sir Reginald Bradbury-Scott. Sometimes it is necessary to cull members of the herd when they become old, ill, or a danger to others. I do not regret my actions."' Moore shook his head. 'Well, I suppose that's *that*, then. Case closed.'

PC McKinnon squeezed in, peering over Moore's shoulder and pointing at the suicide note. 'Look, he's quoted a bit of poetry, but it's wrong:

"Ours is not to reason why,
Ours is but to do and die."'

He shook his head. 'Should be:

"Theirs not to make reply,
Theirs not to reason why,
Theirs but to do and die,
Into the valley of Death
Rode the six hundred."'

A nod. '"The Charge of the Light Brigade", Alfred Lord Tennyson, born 1809, died 1892.' McKinnon shrugged as they stared at him. 'Did it for my English higher.'

Moore put the note back on the table. 'We'll need a forensic graphographer to make sure it's his handwriting. Maybe take fingerprints.'

'Aye, well, I think we're pretty sure it's genuine. Look.' Roberta nodded at the mantelpiece. The remains of a fire were cold and grey in the grate, but above it sat Albert Nairn's very last tableau – a little gallows with a mouse-version of himself hanging from it. Two other figures were gathered around it, looking up at the tiny dead body. Another mouse in a high-vis jacket and a small weasel. The weasel had the same jacket on, but its hair was stuck-on sticky-out badger fur, just like the mini-me he'd given her yesterday.

'Wow.' Moore whistled, low and slow. 'He *did* say you weren't a mouse.'

McKinnon's bottom lip poked out, his face all kicked puppy-dog.

She gave him another thump. 'What's crawled up your bum?'

'Why didn't he make one of *me*?'

'Because nobody cares and you're a whinge. Now go see if you can find a sheet or a blanket, or something. We'll have to cut him down and haul him back to the hotel. Stick him in the fridge too.' She puffed out a breath. 'Rate we're going, the damn thing's going to be stuffed full of dead bodies by the time Inverness get here.'

The expedition back to the hotel had turned into a rather sad-but-surreal dubstep concert – the *wub-wonk, wub-wonk, wub-wonk...* of Roberta's wellies joined by the *patter-patter-patter...* of falling rain and repetitive *squeal-creak-click, squeal-creak-click, squeal-creak-click...* from the buggy's rusty wheels.

About twice the size of a wheelbarrow, with big fat tyres, liberated from behind Nairn's cottage by Sergeant Moore.

He laboured away, hauling the thing along the path, with its owner's earthly remains slumped inside. They'd wrapped him in a couple of itchy MOD-style blankets, in a dysentery-shade of khaki brown – like a miserable burrito – leaving the rope around his throat to keep whatever pathologist they got lumbered with happy.

PC McKinnon marched at the head of their column this time, Nairn's rifle at parade rest over one shoulder, and the shotgun broken in the crook of his other arm. Very pleased with himself, like Mummy's Little Soldier.

Stuck at the back, Roberta frowned at the wrapped body. 'Does this not all seem a bit … convenient to you?'

Moore shrugged. 'Not very convenient for Albert Nairn.'

Suppose not.

But still…

All those loose ends, neatly tied up. No need to investigate any further, officers, why not sit down and have a nice cup of tea instead? Forget aaaaaaaaall about it.

Moore stopped and she came within an inch of marching into the back of the cart. He was standing there, looking at her.

'What?'

'I said, at least we can stop cooping people up in their rooms now.'

'Oh.' She chewed on the inside of her cheek for a bit. 'No.'

'But Nairn's dead. He killed Sir Reginald, so—'

'Everyone stays cooped up till we've interviewed the lot of them. This doesn't stop being a murder inquiry, just because the main suspect's killed himself.'

'But—'

'No. Now get pulling.'

Moore rolled his eyes, turned, picked up the buggy's handles and hauled it down the track again.

Wub-wonk, wub-wonk, wub-wonk…
Patter-patter, patter-patter, patter-patter, patter-patter…
Squeal-creak-click, squeal-creak-click, squeal-creak-click…

It had a beat, but you couldn't dance to it.

Sergeant Moore tucked their khaki bundle onto the shelf under Sir Reginald's. Even in death, the gamekeeper looked like a lower-class version of the toff above him. No crisp white sheet for Albert Nairn, just some manky old army blankets covered in dead animal hair.

Moore straightened up, rubbing the small of his back. 'You sure we can't just—'

'Positive.' She marched out of the fridge. 'Get yourself into dry clothes and we'll start on the second half of your list.'

Because one thing was certain – there was something rotten in the heart of Skirivour and she was going to find out *what* if it killed her.

Or everyone else.

18

The tumble-drier warmth faded from her jeans, socks, and pants, as Roberta perched on the end of the bed in 'Auchentoshan'. Not a double, this time, but two singles with matching tartan bedding. Like the pair of middle-aged biddies who scowled back at her every time she asked a question. Dorothy and Edith Gladstone.

No wonder her pants had gone cold – these two could suck the life out of a hedgehog at fifty paces.

Their hair was dyed an identical brassy blonde. Matching twinsets and pearls. Even their glasses were the same. One sitting in the armchair by the window, the other standing behind it with a hand on her doppelganger's shoulder. It gave them a kind of 'Hinge and Bracket, the early years' look.

'I see.' Sergeant Moore wrote something in his notebook, looked at Dorothy, or was it Edith? 'And what about you, Mrs Gladstone?'

'It's *Miss*, you imbecile.' The one in the armchair stuck her chin out. 'And my sister's just been over this, weren't you paying attention?'

The other Miss Gladstone – definitely Edith, she looked like an Edith – nodded. 'It's beyond the pale, it really is. We've been cooped up in here all morning and all yesterday too!'

'Even *criminals* are allowed out to the exercise yard for an hour a day!'

'We're on the Scottish Penal Reform Association board, you know.'

Dorothy narrowed her eyes. 'And we shall be writing a *very* scathing letter to your superiors about this.'

Of course they would.

Roberta hopped down from the bed and scuffed over to the tea-and-coffee-making facilities. Ooh, they hadn't eaten their biscuits. More fool them.

She helped herself to a wee individually-wrapped lemon-and-white-chocolate shortbread finger. Spraying citrusy crumbs. 'You haven't got any custard creams stashed, have you?'

Both Miss Gladstones stuck their noses in the air, as if she'd never spoken.

Sergeant Moore tapped his notepad. 'If we could get back to the topic of Sir Reginald Bradbury-Scott?'

'*Such* a tragedy.' Edith dabbed at her eye with a lace handkerchief. 'Good old Sir Reginald.'

Dorothy sat forward. 'He was a real character, you know.'

A nod from her sister. 'A real character.'

Not this *again*.

Roberta curled forward and banged her head off the sideboard, hard enough to make the wood boom. 'Aaaaargh!'

'Is she always this uncouth, or have you had her specially trained?'

'Tamdhu':

Edmund Blacklock was in his mid-fifties, trying to look early-twenties and not really managing it in chinos and a denim shirt that paunched out over his belt. The Michael-Portillo hair didn't help.

His wife really *was* in her early-twenties, but somehow,

some evil bastard had managed to convince her that 'Princess Diana tribute act' was a good look.

Edmund struck a Churchillian pose. At least he had the jowls for it. 'There's no doubt in my mind that Sir Reginald was the *salt* of the earth. Isn't that right, Letitia?'

She burst into rapturous applause. 'Oh well said, Edmund, well said!'

'Knockando':

Hats off to her: Mrs Euphemia De Belleforte was rocking the whole Cougar-auditioning-for-a-reality-TV-show-where-she-gets-to-seduce-middle-aged-police-officers thing. Flashing heaps of quivering cleavage as she fluttered her eyelashes at Sergeant Moore. 'Oh yes, dear, *dear*, Reggie. He was such a card…'

Out on the balcony, Roberta leaned forward and boinked her forehead off the wooden handrail, once for every repetition: '"Salt of the earth."' *Boink*. '"A real character."' *Boink*. '"Such a card."' *Boink*.

There was an embarrassed sounding 'Ahem.' And when she peeled open one eye, there was PC McKinnon, looking at her as if she'd done something weird and/or terrible.

'What do *you* want?'

He pulled a face at Sergeant Moore. 'Is she OK?'

'Not entirely sure how to answer that one, Mikey.'

Roberta straightened up. 'Every single bloody one of them.' She hauled in a deep breath and bellowed it out into the cavernous lobby: '"SALT OF THE EARTH!"' The echoes didn't last long – swallowed up by the stuffed animals, oil paintings, and tapestries.

McKinnon grimaced. 'Maybe her blood sugar's low? Been a while since lunch, and carrot pâté with turnip compote and venison gel doesn't exactly fill you up, does it?'

She slapped her hand down on the rail. 'It's like they've all rehearsed their statements! How can one man, one *massive dick* of a man, be universally loved by all these …' She screwed her face up. 'Tory *twats*?'

'Erm…'

Roberta turned and jabbed PC McKinnon with a finger. 'You told me he screwed everyone over!'

'I said, "probably not his friends", though.' Backing away, hands up. Surrendering.

'Aaaaargh!'

Sergeant Moore stared at the pointy metal antlers. 'Maybe Mikey's right? You don't crap in your own nest, do you.'

The wee loon nodded. 'Nope. You poop over the edge of it. Make sure it lands on somebody else. Someone *beneath* you.'

'Very true, Mikey.' He was obviously trying to sound reasonable, but it just came off as patronising. 'And if he thought they all hated him, why would he invite them to his daughter's wedding? You any idea how much this shindig must've cost?'

Pair of idiots. 'He was *rubbing it in*! It's a power thing with old gits like him; "keep your enemies closer".' How could they not see that?

'Didn't work out too well, though, did it?'

'Gah…' She covered her face with her hands. 'How many more of these scumbags have we got to interview?'

'One more guest, nine members of staff.'

Roberta let her hands fall to her sides and sagged there for a bit. 'Why does the universe hate me?'

McKinnon shuffled his trainers. 'At least we're doing something, right? We're *trying*.'

'And achieving bugger all!' She gave the balustrade a kick. The statue a scowl. An oil painting the Vs. Then turned and marched away.

PC McKinnon and Sergeant Moore hurried after her, the wee loon doing his best to look keen and determined. 'Where are we going?'

'I'm sick of interviewing monkeys – time to go see the organ grinder!'

The door lay at the end of a slightly tatty wee corridor – the tartan carpet scuffed and faded, its walls in need of a fresh coat of paint and someone to fix that damp patch on the ceiling. Like the hotel laundry, it hadn't merited a fancy whisky name. Instead a simple brass plaque with, 'Private Residence' was screwed above a letterbox.

All very low key.

Roberta fiddled with Old Faithful, working its wandering underwire into a slightly less pokey position as Sergeant Moore raised his hand to knock.

'I swear, if one more of these buggers says, "he was a real character"…'

Moore sighed. 'Still think you're making a rod for yourself. Nairn's dead, we don't have to—'

'Aye, we sodding well do.'

'All right, all right.' Hands up. 'How about this, then: we get this one done, then go have afternoon tea or something? Little finger sandwiches, that kind of stuff. Bet they've got loads of leftover wedding cake.' He tried for a smile. 'You'll like that, won't you? Cake?'

'I'm no' six, you patronising cockspanner! Knock on the bloody door.'

'Only trying to help.' He gave the wood a traditional police triple.

'And they *better* have cake.'

God this was taking forever. What the hell was the old—

A clunk – like a deadbolt being released – and the door swung open, revealing Lord Oliver William Fitzroy-Galbraith in all his disapproving glory. He'd ditched last night's paisley-patterned PJs and dressing gown for red corduroy trousers and one of those ugly checked shirts beloved of farmers, people *pretending* to be farmers, and dickheads. Given that he'd topped the outfit off with a polka-dot cravat, there were no prizes for guessing which one *he* was.

Lord Sharny-Bumflaps looked them up and down, curling his lip when he got to Roberta. 'I assume you're here to apologise for your terrible behaviour yesterday morning?'

'Official business.' She flashed her out-of-date warrant card. 'We need to talk to you about your old mate Sir Reginald Bradbury-Scott. Deceased. And your other old mate, Albert Nairn. *Also* deceased. Bit of a coincidence, eh?'

That made the temperature drop a bit.

'I see.'

Sergeant Moore nodded towards the private apartments. 'So, Your Lordship, if you don't mind, that is?'

'Hmph...' He turned. 'I suppose you'd better follow me.'

They did, into a room that seemed to have escaped whichever tartan-obsessed monster had been allowed to run rampant through the rest of the hotel. But compared to the guests' rooms, it was all a bit shabby in here. The sofa and armchairs sagged like an old cat's belly. Faded rugs on the floor *almost* managing to hide bald patches in the ancient carpet. Wallpaper that had seen better decades, never mind days. Window frames that needed painting...

Even the view was crap: overlooking what had to be the kitchen roof, extractor-fan outlets dotting it like manky mushrooms. Out across a dip of soggy grass, then nothing but miserable grey rain-battered trees.

And for some reason, Roberta couldn't help but smile.

'Schadenfreude' was a lovely word, wasn't it?

Sergeant Moore scribbled away in his notebook, sitting in a wingback chair whose stuffing was making a bid for freedom. Writing everything down, as if Lord Fitzroy-Galbraith was saying anything in the least bit useful to their investigation.

Roberta slouched back on the couch, one leg swinging as the interview stretched on into mind-numbing eternity.

'It's a terrible shame about Nairn. He was an excellent gamekeeper, led record-breaking shoots every Glorious Twelfth. Don't know who'll raise the pheasants now. You see, running a shooting estate takes a lot more work than people realise...'

Blah, blah, blah, blah, blah.

On and on and on.

Look at him, standing there in the middle of the room with his hands clasped behind his back, as if he was still in the military. With his silly military moustache and shiny military shoes. Wanging on about how you couldn't get decent staff any more, because people just didn't know their place.

And what was with the name? Lord Oliver William Fitzroy-Galbraith. Why did these posh sods have to hyphenate everything? Did they think it made them sound more important? Oh, your surname doesn't have a hyphen in it? You must be one of those *lower* classes one hears about!

Mind you, Susan and Roberta had done the same with the kids: Jasmine and Naomi Wallace-Steel. But that was *different*, and not rampant hypocrisy *at all*. Because they weren't posh tossers.

Or something.

Ahem...

Anyway, the French had the right idea: march all your aristocrats up to Madame Guillotine and chop their heads off. *Thunk*. Crowd cheers. Everyone goes home for baguettes, stinky cheese, and a bonk. Sometimes you just had to learn the lessons of history. March 'em up, chop 'em off. And not just the aristos, either – the world would be a much better place if two-thirds of its political class suddenly became ten-inches shorter. Then there were the people who didn't indicate at roundabouts. Or pronounced Glenmorangie, 'Glen-mor-ANNE-jee'. And what about—

'I *beg* your pardon?'

Roberta blinked and there was His Lordship, treating Sergeant Moore to an imperious sneer.

Fitzroy-Galbraith folded his arms. 'Did he have any enemies? *Reginald*? Enemies?'

God, the landed gentry loved the sound of their own voices.

She sat up. 'Any chance you can answer the question instead of repeating it?'

'Did Reginald have any enemies? Well, Albert Nairn *killed* him, so I'm guessing he probably *did*!' A haughty sniff. 'What a stupid question. You don't get to *be* an MP without knifing people in the back, and you certainly don't get to *stay* one without knifing even more. Then burying the bodies. And pinning the blame on someone else.' He marched over to the window and stood there with his back to the room, staring down at the kitchens. 'Half the village hated him, and the other half loathed him. He played them for idiots with that

Skirivour Goldmine Association thing. Not *just* them, I'm sorry to say.'

Ooh, now they were getting somewhere.

'He play you?'

'I am Lord Oliver William Fitzroy-Galbraith,' the words hard and clipped, '*no one* plays me.'

'If you didn't like him, how come you let him have his daughter's wedding here?'

The old git tutted, like it was the stupidest question he'd ever heard. 'Do you have any idea what the upkeep on a place like this is? Running an ancestral pile is crippling; the arrangement was purely financial.'

'Didn't look like that during the speeches, Friday night. Looked like the two of you were total BFFs.'

A short and bitter laugh barked out into the shabby room. 'A wise man knows when to grease the wheels, Detective Chief Inspector, especially when they belong to your local MP and the man has discretion regarding … certain planning applications, grants, funding, and initiatives.'

So she'd been right: friends close, enemies closer.

What was it Susan had been going on about at dinner last night? Holiday homes and high-end villas?

Even *more* interesting.

'Oh aye: "planning applications"?' Roberta raised her eyebrows. 'Care to elaborate on that?'

'No, I would not.'

The carriage clock on the mantelpiece ticked, getting louder as the silence stretched. Rain battered the window.

Sergeant Moore cleared his throat, pen poised and ready.

But Lord Fitzroy-Galbraith just stood there, hands clasped behind his back, scowling down at the kitchen and its mushroomy extractor-fan outlets.

OK…

She settled into the couch again. 'What about affairs? Wee birdie tells me our boy Sir Reggie was a bit free and easy where he tossed the old family caber?'

That got her an imperious sniff. 'I'll leave the Sergeant to answer that one, I don't lower myself to backstairs gossip.' He checked his watch. 'Now, if there's nothing else, I have more important things to do than waste my time with your puerile questions. Albert Nairn killed Sir Reginald: you have his confession. This matter is now *closed*.' A long thin finger came up and pointed at the door. 'You may go.'

Aye, that'll be shining.

Sergeant Moore stood, but Roberta stayed where she was.

'Quick question for you: if you could describe Sir Reginald in one simple phrase, what would it be?'

Lord Fitzroy-Galbraith turned, nose in the air. '"*Caveat emptor*" springs to mind.'

'Ah.' Moore nodded. '"Let the buyer beware..."'

Yes, thank you Dictionary Corner.

Roberta stood. 'No' "salt of the earth"?'

'Salt is a *useful* thing, Detective Chief Inspector, but too much can be *very* bad for your health.'

19

Rain snapped and popped against the library windows, wind mourning at the joints in the woodwork, while the sky hung there, murderous and dark. Letting only the meanest light spill into the gloomy room.

The weird wee redhead, Janey, had served Roberta's teeny Major Investigation Team afternoon tea, done a weird wee curtsey, holding down the hem of her weird wee tartan miniskirt, then made her weird wee self scarce before Roberta could point out that what Skirivour Castle Hotel billed as 'serves three' was barely enough for one.

Roberta plucked the last cucumber-and-cream-cheese from the crumb-speckled platter and stuffed it in her dinner-hole. Crunchy and soft and creamy and delicious AND TOO BLOODY SMALL.

PC McKinnon must have seen her eyeing the last inch of his ham-and-mustard, because he wolfed it down before she could nab it. Greedy sod. His words had to fight their way around the miniature mouthful. 'Is it wrong I'm a bit disappointed we got through the whole thing with only two dead bodies? If this was on the telly we'd have at least three more murders by now. And maybe a car chase? Ooh! I know: or someone *vanishing* into the woods, leaving nothing behind but a mysterious note...'

'Yes, it's *wrong*.' Sergeant Moore leaned forward in his

armchair, setting free a squeaky-leather farting noise, and topped up everyone's china cups from a pot the size of his head. It was the only thing the hotel had been generous with.

Well, except for the wedding cake. And that didn't count, because the father-of-the-bride would've paid for it in advance, and being dead he wasn't in any position to complain about them doling out the leftovers willy-nilly. A small mountain of it, all cut into rectangles and piled on a plate, sat in the middle of the coffee table like sticky dot-less dominos.

'You know what bothers me?' Roberta helped herself to a domino of cake. 'Only person in the whole place who'll admit to no' liking the old bugger is the one person you'd think would stick up for him.' She pulled her mouth out and down, in a proper disgusted-frog face. 'As for the rest of them…?'

'Salt of the earth.' Sergeant Moore did the honours with the milk. 'Such a card. A real character.'

'It really *is* like they've been rehearsing their statements. Or someone's coached them.' She took a bite of sweet sticky brown cake, knocking the icing free. 'Mmmm, cake.' All those dates and sultanas and raisins, all working together in one sticky gooey…

She stopped chewing and frowned.

Then stood and scuffed her way across the tartan carpet to where the library doors sat in a recess, just wide and deep enough to accommodate a small antique table. A hotel phone sat on top of it, nearly as big as the one at reception – probably down to the fact that they'd named the rooms after single malts, instead of numbering the bloody things like anyone with half a brain would've, so each button had the name of a whisky attached to it.

Sergeant Moore watched her go. 'It doesn't really matter though, does it? Albert Nairn killed Sir Reginald, it was right there in his suicide note. The rest of them might be rancid Tory dickheads, but at least they haven't killed anyone.'

McKinnon helped himself to cake. 'Wasn't just Sir Reginald he killed. Completely murdered that poem.'

She picked up the receiver and pressed the button marked 'Lagavulin'.

Silence.

OK, that was a relief, for a moment there she—

Susan's voice burst from the earpiece. *'Hello?'*

Of course it was.

Roberta closed her eyes and pulled her lips back from her teeth, trying to hold the swearing in.

'Hello? Is anyone there?'

Stay calm. Don't shout. Nice and nonchalant. Forcing as much jollity into it as possible with a clenched jaw. 'Aye, just wanted to make sure you're still OK.'

A wee hint of saucy minx flirted its way into Roberta's ear. *'Why don't you come up here and find out for yourself? I might have been* very *naughty.'*

Stay calm.

'Good. I'll ... talk to you later.'

'Love you.'

STAY CALM.

'Me too.' Roberta placed the handset back into its cradle with slow deliberation. Backed away from the antique, and probably very *expensive* table, then growled like a pissed-off tiger, flinging her arms and legs about as the growl built to a throat-rattling, 'AAAAAAAAAAAAAAAAAAARGH!' Blood pounding in her face and neck, spittle flying as she thrashed.

Sergeant Moore scrambled to his feet. 'Are you OK?'

'DO I SODDING *LOOK* OK?' Trembling with the effort of bottling it all back up again. Hissing out sizzling breaths. 'The *internal phone lines* have been working all the sodding time! It's just *outside* you can't call. You can chat room-to-room to your nasty little heart's content.' A deep breath. 'AAAAAAAA-AAAAAAAAAAAAARRRRRRGH!'

'Why are you...?' His mouth fell open as his brain finally caught up. '"Like they've been rehearsing their statements."'

PC McKinnon's eyes widened – always last to the thinky party. 'Maybe Agatha Christie was right after all? All them people, working together...'

Like the dates, sultanas, and raisins in the wedding cake. Only instead of sticky gooey deliciousness, they were working on a murder.

Sergeant Moore shook his head. 'I hate to rain on your Miss Marple Appreciation Society parade, but Albert Nairn killed—'

'What if it wasn't *just* him? What if he had help?' Roberta slumped against the wall and stared at the ceiling for a bit.

Well, there was nothing else for it, was there?

'All right.' She marched back to the coffee table, snatched another bit of cake from the plate and jammed it in her gob. Spraying dark brown angry crumbs. 'If it's Agatha Christie they want, it's Agatha Christie they'll bloody well get!'

PC McKinnon bustled out into the lobby, rubbing his hands and nodding. 'That's everyone.'

Roberta stuck her head around the door and peered into the library.

The room wasn't exactly *full*, full, but it was getting there. Forty-nine people milled about as Sergeant Moore shepherded them all down to one end. Thirty-seven guests and twelve members of hotel staff, all looking a lot less pyjama-and-nightdressy than they had last time they were gathered together for roll-call at three o'clock that morning.

A low background murmur oozed out of the gathering: It's such a terrible shock. Isn't it a shame about poor old Sir Reginald? Who would have thought it? The gamekeeper! Isn't Lady Bradbury-Scott holding up well. It's Adriana and Douglas I feel sorry for – a murder and a suicide, at their *wedding*, I mean to say...

None of them seemed to notice that all the curtains were drawn, shutting out the thin grey light.

Her Ladyship had pride of place on a large leather sofa, brought in from one of the other rooms specially for the occasion. A middle-aged fat man sat on her left, both hands clasped in front of his tweed three-piece suit, Adriana on her right. There wasn't any room for Douglas Moore on the sofa, so he stood behind his new wife – one hand on her shoulder, still posing for that photoshoot.

Lord Fitzroy-Galbraith perched himself in an armchair, pulled up next to the sofa, arms resting on the silver handle of a walking stick. Imperious and every inch the patriarch.

Gathered together like that, the five of them looked like something out of *Grimmer Homes and Tories*. Or a really nasty episode of *Game of Thrones*. Which probably amounted to much the same thing, only with less full-frontal nudity and more backstabbing.

Weird Wee Janey had clearly been in again, because a tray of tea and cake was set on the coffee table in front of the VIPs.

Even Susan was there, standing off to one side, by the Barbara Cartlands. Shuffling her feet, all on her own, abandoned by work colleagues and – God forbid – friends.

Sergeant Moore glanced towards the door and Roberta gave him the nod.

'ALL RIGHT, EVERYONE!' Raising his arms and voice till they settled into an uneasy silence.

She turned to PC McKinnon, barely whispering so none of the other buggers could overhear. 'You got it?'

The wee spud looked a bawhair off wetting himself with excitement as he pointed at the switches just inside the door. But at least he kept it quiet: 'Soon as you get to the dramatic bit, I kill the lights.'

'Good boy.' Surely even *he* couldn't cock that up?

Roberta dipped into her pocket and produced the wee jar of hand cream she'd pilfered from Susan's make-up bag fifteen minutes ago. Glass, about the size of a hockey puck, with an unpronounceable name and bum-clenching price tag.

She turned it over in her fingers.

This was going to work. Of course it was.

Always worked for Miss Marple...

Come on then.

Roberta marched into the library, and every face in the room turned to watch her.

She stopped beside Sergeant Moore, hands in her pockets, a wee bit slouchy, in contrast to his parade-rest pose. Maybe a wee bit more Columbo than Miss Marple, then. But a *sexy* Columbo, so that was OK.

Big smile. 'I suppose you're all wondering why I've gathered you here today.'

Standing in the doorway, McKinnon gave her a cheesy grin and two thumbs up.

Ah, maybe he wasn't such a bad wee lump after all?

'As you know—'

'Oh, do speak up!' Bloody Lord Fitzroy-Galbraith shifted in his armchair. 'I can't abide mumbling.'

Rotten fusty old sod did that on purpose.

She started again, louder and harder this time. And more than a little hacked off. '*As you know*: Sir Reginald Bradbury-Scott was murdered at some point between the wedding reception and half four Saturday morning. We believe he probably died from a blow to the back of the head.'

A Mexican wave of fake-startled-gasping rippled through the crowd.

Lying bastards.

'A blow to the head that—'

'Oh, for goodness' sake.' Lord Fusty-Bumcrack thumped the tip of his walking stick against the floor. 'This is all immaterial. Albert Nairn was a hardworking and conscientious gamekeeper, but he snapped and for some reason known only to him, decided to kill Sir Reginald. It – was – in – his – suicide – note.' Saying it slow and clear, so the silly old police officers could understand.

She gave him a cold smile. 'If you wouldn't mind hudding your wheesht for five minutes, Your Lordship, maybe you'll find out why it's *not* immaterial at all. In fact, it's very material *indeed*.' Stared him down till he sat back in his armchair again.

'Very well, proceed.' As if *he* was the one in charge here.

'Sir Reginald was killed by a blow to the head, right here.' Roberta tapped herself on the noggin, right where she'd found the broken-Easter-egg bit on the body's skull. 'This implies his killer came at him from behind. His *left-handed* killer.' She did one of those theatrical hand gestures, as if she was introducing a magic trick. 'And would anyone like to guess if Albert Nairn was left-handed or right-handed? Anyone? He was *right*-handed, unlike our killer.'

This time the shocked gasping sounded a lot more authentic.

'Our killer who set Albert Nairn up, and probably killed him too. Made it look like a suicide so we'd stop investigating. They thought they'd planned for every eventuality. They thought they'd got away with it. But our killer made one *fatal* mistake.' She left a pause – one hairy bumhole, two hairy bumholes, three hairy bumholes – milking it. Quick glance to make sure PC McKinnon had his finger on the switch. Then, 'A killer who I can now reveal to be...!'

McKinnon switched the lights off, plunging the room into darkness.

A scream rang out from the crowd, followed by another one, then the ringing crash of something metal hitting the floor, and the high-pinging-crackle of shattering porcelain. Which set off more screaming.

Exactly as planned.

'Lights, Constable!'

They flickered on again ... but everyone was still right where they'd been before the lights went out. The only thing that'd changed was the tray of tea things wasn't on the coffee table any more – it was spread in jagged shards all over the tartan carpet, bits of cake everywhere.

'Oh.' She frowned at what was left of the teapot. 'Now, you see, that should've worked.' Then at Sergeant Moore. 'It always works in crime novels.'

Lord Fitzroy-Galbraith banged his stick on the floor again, just to make sure *he* was the centre of attention. Poncy show-off. 'Are we done with this ridiculous charade, now?'

Were they hell.

'Simon says, "Everyone who's left-handed: stick that sinister paw of yours in the air."'

Not a single hand went up.

So Roberta put a bit of force behind it. 'Come on, folks, SIMON SAYS!'

Finally, hands reached up above the crowd. Only three of them, though. The VIPs at the front just stared at her – like she needed scraping off the sole of their shoes. Well, that was about to change.

She grinned at them. 'Think fast!' Then pulled the jar of hand cream from her pocket and hurled it at Lady

Bradbury-Scott in a perfect flat arc, heading right for that prissy mug of hers.

Her Ladyship flinched back, hands curled in front of her chest, oh God, it was going to smack her right in the—

Her daughter's hand flashed out and the hand cream slapped into her palm inches from Mummy Dearest's nose. Her daughter's *left* hand.

The plan had worked after all.

Roberta smiled. 'Interesting…'

Adriana rolled her eyes. 'Don't be absurd. My mother and I both wear our watches on our right wrists, of *course* we're left-handed. We never said we weren't.' She turned to scan the crowd, until she was staring straight at Susan, her voice a withering sneer. 'You never told me your wife was a *complete* idiotfest.'

Susan blushed and looked away.

A triumphant sniff, and Adriana twisted the lid off the hand cream and dabbed a little on the back of her hand. Smoothed it in.

Sergeant Moore's mouth barely moved as his voice dropped to a whisper. 'It rubs the lotion on its skin, or else it gets the hose again.'

Adriana went in for a second fingertipful.

Oh, you think so, do you?

Roberta marched right over there and stuck her hand under the cow's nose. Filling the words with menace: 'That's no' yours. *Give.*'

Silence settled back into the room.

Adriana glared at her, all high and haughty. Chin up. So superior.

Roberta bared her teeth.

Oh, if she thought she was going to get away with treating Susan like that, and stealing Susan's *hand cream* like that, and being an utter bitch in front of everyone. *Like. That.* She was about to find out how a four-knuckle sandwich tasted.

Five.

Four.

Three...

Adriana dropped her gaze and held the hand cream out.

Better.

Roberta plucked it from her fingers, tossed it in the air – so everyone could see – and caught it again. Turned her back on the lot of them. 'See, our killer thought they could muddy the water so much, no one would ever see the bottom.' A sigh as she slipped the hand cream back into her pocket. 'Laying a false trail here, distracting with flashy footwork there.' Sauntering back to the middle of the room. 'They say it takes a village to raise a child, but how many people does it take to kill *one* man?'

She turned, nice and slow. For some reason, no one wanted to make eye contact with her. Not even the VIPs. 'Because sooner or later the phones will start working again and, if the bridge is still out, Inverness will send a helicopter full of officers. You'll all be questioned again, under oath this time, *separately*.' Roberta let them think about that for a moment.

A bit of shuffling at the back.

A woman in twinset-and-pearls let loose a little nervous laugh – Edith or Dorothy, it was difficult to tell from here.

A couple of people cleared their throats.

And still no one could look at her.

'Three men can keep a secret as long as two of them are dead, right? Someone *will* crack, they always do. Someone will crack and cut a deal, and then it'll be too late for the rest of you.'

Lord Fitzroy-Galbraith's face wrinkled into a mask of upper-class scorn. 'We don't have to sit here listening to this poppycock.'

'So the choice is: save yourself, or sit at home waiting for that patented knock on your door.' She raised the heel of her boot and hammered it into the carpet – three times, setting the floor booming. Deep breath. 'POLICE! OPEN UP!'

'You don't have any proof anyone's done anything.'

She nodded. 'Oh aye, I do.' Then turned to Sergeant Moore. 'Don't I, *Sergeant*?'

He opened his mouth ... then closed it again. Turned to look at her. 'I... What?'

Roberta tapped herself on the head again, only round the front this time. 'See, my little grey cells have been working away like busy, busy bees the whole time. You argued and argued that we had to move the body, didn't you? Because you knew your DNA would be all over it from when you stuck him up there. *Now* you can claim cross-contamination. Same with Albert Nairn's "suicide" confession that you so *conveniently* found.'

His eyebrows pinched up in the middle. Took him a while, but it finally looked like he'd twigged this was an accusation, not a call for backup. 'That's not—'

'You said you'd never seen *Silence of the Lambs*, but you can quote it, can't you? We all heard you do it.'

Sergeant Moore pulled his chin in. 'Yeah, but everyone can quote—'

'*You* killed Sir Reginald Bradbury-Scott. *You* put those panties in his mouth.' There was another round of shocked gasps at that little revelation. '*You* stuck him on those antlers. Big strong guy like you – used to mountain climbing, rugby, and shinty? Must've been a doddle carrying Sir Reginald up that ladder. And then you killed Albert Nairn and made it look like a suicide to cover your tracks.'

Moore backed off a step, like she'd offered him a nice steaming hot mug of Ebola. 'You're off your tiny hairy rocker, aren't you?'

'He was shagging your wife, wasn't he? Sir Randy Buggery-Snot was having it away *with your wife.*'

'Philippa would never—'

She closed the gap again. 'And you *knew*. Sitting up there on the top table, at the reception, listening to him gloating about everything he'd achieved. The man who *shagged your wife*, patting your son on the back and grooming him to be a Tory MP?'

'No!' Starting to go a bit red now. 'I didn't kill anyone!'

Roberta poked him. 'How much money did you spaff away on his non-existent goldmine? All of it? Everything you'd saved up for your retirement?'

Sergeant Moore squared his shoulders, face darkening. 'Will you *listen* to me?'

'He took everything from you: your wife, your son, your money, your dignity. What else were you going to do, let him get away with it? *Of course* you killed him, and you killed Albert Nairn too!' She raised her finger and poked him again. Hard. 'And I'm going to make sure you go down for sixteen to life.'

20

Everyone stared.

'THAT'S ENOUGH!' Lady Bradbury-Scott rose from the sofa. 'Leave him alone.'

Sitting next to her, Adriana put a hand on her mother's arm. Voice low and warning. 'Mother…' But she was shaken off.

Her Ladyship straightened her broad shoulders, chin up, tall and regal. 'Sandy didn't kill Reginald, *I* did.'

'Mother!'

Sergeant Moore blinked at her. 'Jocasta, don't!'

'It was an accident. He came in, drunk from the wedding, fell and hit his head on the bath.'

Oh, aye, *that* was plausible.

Roberta didn't bother suppressing the laugh. 'What, and then magicked himself up onto that statue? Do I look like I floated down the Dee on an unbuttered dildo?'

She waved that away. 'Nairn said he would dispose of the remains. I suppose he couldn't resist the urge to create one of his silly little tableaus on a more dramatic scale.'

Adriana sighed, then stood. 'Mother's only covering for *me*. I discovered Daddy had embezzled hundreds of thousands from party campaign coffers. *Complete* shamefest. When I confronted him, he threatened to sabotage Douglas's political career if I told anyone. We struggled and he fell.'

Douglas stepped out from behind the sofa and took his

new wife's hand. '*Actually*, darling, I think you'll find it was *me* who struggled with him, when I came to your aid. And *then* he fell and hit his head.' Douglas raised his chin, playing to the crowd. 'It was a tragic stroke of bad luck, but I *truly* believe he would have preferred death to the ignominy of the headlines when it got out he'd betrayed our *beloved* Conservative Party.'

Someone in the back actually clapped.

'Oh Jesus, no' this…' Roberta stepped away from Sergeant Moore and glowered at the lot of them. 'Do you think this is some sort of *joke*? Two men are dead!'

The last one on the couch levered his fat bum upright, took a deep breath and straightened his three-piece tweeds. 'No, *I* killed Father.' Tears sparkled on those chubby cheeks. 'I had enough of the pain he'd put Mother through. The man was a *monster*!'

'Eef I can make *small* statement.' The wee Russian pushed his way to the front of the crowd. 'Friday night, I see Meester Bradbury-Scott trip and fall down all the stairs. Was terrible accident. Very shocking to me.'

Agatha Beresford stepped forward, clutching her husband's hand. 'No, it was us. He robbed Mortimer of his chance of an OBE!'

Susan's boss nodded. 'Man was an absolute stinker of the first water.'

A voice from the back: 'Hear, hear!'

'Actually,' Mr Reeves shook his head, pulling himself up to his full half-sooked lollypop-height, 'it was me that killed the chap, and me alone. I shan't say why, but it was a matter of honour. I'm responsible, not this good lady!'

Agatha beamed at him. 'Oh, you are *sweet*, Hugo.'

It was a proper sodding garden party in here.

Roberta thumped her boot heel into the carpet again.

'Enough of the "I'm Spartacus" bollocks! It doesn't matter how much of a shite he was, you don't get to kill him!'

Everyone looked at her like she'd just crapped in the punchbowl.

Then the lights flickered a couple of times and the library was plunged into darkness again.

Idiots! Why did she always have to work with idiots?

She turned to PC McKinnon. 'No' now, you snot-brained sheep-shagging halfwit!'

'It wasn't me! Generator must've run out of diesel.'

Lord Fitzroy-Galbraith sat forward in his armchair, leaning on the head of that silver walking stick of his, eyes glittering in the dark like a rat's. A razor smile clear in his voice. 'You seem to have an embarrassment of confessions, Detective Chief Inspector. And you can't arrest *everyone*.'

'You bloody watch me!'

A hard, white circle of light burst into the library, sweeping across the carpet till it found Roberta, making her glow like she was centre stage. PC McKinnon shuffled in after it. 'Erm, there *is* another option. If you're interested?' He let his torch beam drift across the shelves of books. 'Only, after you were banging on about *Murder on the Orient Express*, I found it in the library.' The torchlight came to rest on the crime section. 'I skiffed through to the end, cos, you know, not really my kind of thing, but I thought ... maybe ... we could do what Hercule Poirot does?'

How was *that* a reasonable suggestion?

'Hercule...?' She thumped him. 'This is real life, Constable, no' a Golden-Age crime novel!'

'Ow!' He backed off a pace and the torch focussed on her again. 'No, but *maybe* I saw a broken window round the back of the property when I was looking earlier? So *what if* someone broke into the hotel Friday night, under cover of the storm, and murdered Sir Reginald? Then, you know, hung his body up on the statue, and disappeared off into the night before the bridge collapsed?'

Lord Fitzroy-Galbraith's voice stalked out of the darkness, dragging its pink scaly tail with it. 'Or, perhaps, he disappeared *as* the bridge collapsed? Meaning his body's been washed downriver and out to sea, where it will *never* be found. Hmmm… But what about Nairn's confession?'

McKinnon's torch found him in the darkness, the beam wide enough at that distance to illuminate most of the VIP section. 'Maybe no one needs to see it and we can chalk it up to a lonely old man going a bit dotty with all his stuffed weird animals in the woods?'

Lady Bradbury-Scott dabbed at her eye with a hanky. 'So tragic.'

'You know,' the little Russian's voice chipped in from the gloom, 'now I am theenking about it, maybe I *not* see Meester Bradbury-Scott make fall. Maybe I see *shadowy figure* in middle of night?'

'Ooh,' Mortimer Beresford nodded. 'Yes, I think *I* saw that too.'

Then Weird Janey sidled into the torchlight, one hand raised like she was needing a pee. 'I'm sure the sound of broken glass woke me up. Must've been about … three in the morning?'

A man's voice: 'You know, that's just what I remember: smashing glass, three a.m. Coming back to me, bright as day now.'

And before you could say, Lying Bunch Of Utter Bastards, they were all at it, nodding and murmuring in the darkness about how they all remembered the exact same thing.

Roberta bared her teeth again. 'You can't just—'

'I wish to alter my statement.' Lady Bradbury-Scott did that regal thing with her chin again. 'Reginald never came to bed that night, because he was out ... having relations with that floozy parlourmaid of his.' She pointed at Weirdo Janey. 'Her.'

'Hoy!' The redhead's cheeks flushed hot pink. 'I'm a Residents' Hospitality-Experience Manager, not a *parlourmaid*.' Didn't deny the floozy bit, though.

Lady Bradbury-Scott gave her a little bow. 'No offence.' Then turned back to Roberta. 'Sergeant Moore ... *Sandy*, was with me all night after the reception ended and the bar was closed, so he couldn't have had anything to do with Reginald's unfortunate end. Besides, he was *far* too tipsy. And he was with me *last* night as well, so he can't have had anything to do with Albert Nairn's suicide either.' She held her hands out to Sergeant Moore. 'We've been having an affair, and are in love.'

Moore bit his lip, then rushed over and wrapped her up in his arms, framed by torchlight. 'Oh, Jocasta...'

She beamed at him. 'Sandy!'

The pair of them kissed and every bugger in the room applauded, like this was a rom-com instead of a murder inquiry.

'Oh, for God's sake!' Roberta hauled in a deep breath. 'YOU'RE ALL A BUNCH OF UTTER BASTARDS!'

Lord Fitzroy-Galbraith stood. 'Well, I think that concludes our business, ladies and gentlemen. Janey?'

The weird wee redhead curtseyed. 'Yes, Your Lordship?'

'Open the curtains, there's a good girl. And I think we'll have afternoon tea in the conservatory today, shall we?'

Roberta turned on her heel and stormed from the room, slamming the library doors behind her.

She leaned back against the carved grey stonework that flanked the hotel entrance, and took another swig of Glenfeòrag, straight from the bottle. Burping as its smoky burn spread across her chest, warming Old Faithful from the inside.

From here, on the top step, beneath that stone portico, there was a perfect view – if your idea of a perfect view involved lots and lots of grey and rain and trees. Not the comfiest of seats, bit hard on the old arse, but at least she wasn't in there hobnobbing with conniving, lying, murdering, conspiratorial bastards.

Now *that* was something worth drinking to.

So she did.

Should've nabbed some crisps when she liberated the bottle, but there weren't any in the sort-of-locked case it'd been hiding in behind the reception desk. Well, it wasn't like they needed it to welcome anyone, was it? No bugger was turning up till the bridge got fixed, or the phones came back on...

She pulled out her mobile and checked. Nope: still no bars.

No bars and the battery was almost flat too.

But the generator was out of diesel, which meant no lights, no hot food, no hot water, and no way to recharge her e-cigarette either... Unless she siphoned fuel out of those big posh four-by-fours marooned in the overflowing car park? Or broke into someone's Jaguar and hijacked their USB charging port? Which was *definitely* worth a go.

To celebrate, Roberta sooked in a huge breath of cherry vape and hissed it out through her nose. Closing her eyes to enjoy that nicotine and whisky hit.

A creak and a thunk sounded behind her – the hotel door opening and closing again.

'Robbie?' Susan settled down on the top step. Close enough to feel the warmth of her skin.

Roberta kept her eyes on the rain-drenched world. 'Yup.'

'That lanky constable's off breaking a window round the back.' She nudged her. 'Are you all right?'

Course she wasn't.

Another swig of Glenfeòrag, eyes front. 'Did you know?'

'Did I know what?'

Roberta gestured with the bottle, setting its amber contents sloshing. '*This*. Were you part of it? Every other bugger was.'

'Robbie!' Her stern voice. 'Of *course* I wasn't. And you should be ashamed of yourself for even *thinking* that.'

Yeah, well, one more thing that could join the list.

Rain hissed against the gravel, sparked off the loch-sized puddles around Prostate Fountain, growled in the trees.

Off in the middle distance, a fat black crow lifted above the pines, realised it was still pissing down, and sulked back into the forest again. Probably thinking, 'Bugger this for a game of soldiers.' It and her both.

Susan pulled her shoulders up. 'Mortimer's offered me a promotion: partnership in the firm. Comes with a thirty percent pay rise, profit share, and eight weeks' holiday.'

'Going to take it?'

She made a little humming noise. 'Haven't decided. It's a bribe to keep me quiet, obviously, but it's a great opportunity too.' Her shoulder bumped into Roberta's. 'The important thing is: what do *you* want to do?'

'Pff...' Another big lungful of cherry. Holding it in. 'None of the buggers in there are going to admit what really happened, are they? They've got strength in numbers – what've I got?'

'The truth?'

Hard not to laugh at that. 'With no evidence? It's just conjecture and supposition. Sergeant Buggering Moore's compromised all the forensics – the Procurator Fiscal won't touch this one with a stick. You know what PFs are like: "Too difficult to prove criminal conspiracy," she'll say. "Why didn't you just pick someone and beat a confession out of them?"' Roberta plucked a wee nugget of gravel from between her feet and hurled it out into the rain. 'Or they'll just want to pin it on Albert Nairn, and everyone else gets off scot-free.'

The door creaked open again, and there he was: man of the sodding hour.

Sergeant Moore cleared his throat. 'Thought I'd find you here.'

Bet he did.

She took another swig. 'Go away.'

He closed the door behind him and stepped out under the portico. Turned to face her. Standing there with his hands behind his back, like he was reporting for duty and expecting a bollocking.

Roberta pulled on the most disgusted face she could manage. 'So, you got away with murder, then?'

'Honestly, I swear on my kids' lives, I had *nothing* to do with it, OK? Scout's honour.' He did the little salute. 'Cross my heart and hope to get a terrible dose of piles.' He licked his lips in the ensuing silence. Shifted his feet on the gravel. Cleared his throat again. 'It *wasn't* me, and that's the God's honest truth! I did *not* kill Sir Reginald Bradbury-Scott.'

Like that mattered.

'If it wasn't you, it was your recently widowed girlfriend, and you helped her cover it up. Even if his death was an accident, you're both guilty: perverting the course of justice, eight years apiece.'

Sergeant Moore clasped a hand over his heart. 'I had nothing to do with it and neither did Jocasta. We really were together all Friday night. And last night too.' Frown. 'Well, most of it anyway.'

'What I don't get is: why put the body on display like that? Why no' just throw him down the stairs and have done with it? Just making work for yourselves.'

'We've been seeing each other since Philippa left me. And before you ask: no, it wasn't a revenge affair. Philippa wasn't shagging Sir Reginald.' Deep breath. 'The butcher she was sleeping with was a woman. So was the lady who ran the mobile library, the receptionist at our local vet's, and a dental hygienist called Ursula.'

Lucky old Philippa.

Roberta squinted at him, tilting her head to one side. 'Or did you stick him up there because: why wouldn't you? Whole hotel's clarted with dead things. Surprised you didn't have him stuffed and mounted. Albert Nairn would've given you special mates' rates. Then, maybe, you wouldn't have had to kill him too?'

Moore sagged. 'Please, I'm baring my soul here!'

'But, see doing all this when you know there's a police officer here? A *real* police officer, no' a corrupt parochial bunnet like you and that idiot, McKinnon. How arrogant would you have to be?' She took a deep swig of whisky, then handed the bottle to Susan. Making eye contact with Sergeant Moore the whole time, so he'd know he was being snubbed.

Susan frowned at the bottle. 'Why does the label have, "Welcome to Skirivour Castle Hotel" on it?' When she didn't get an answer, she shrugged and knocked back a glug. Squooshing it through her teeth like it was a fine wine before swallowing. 'Not bad.'

'And if that's not enough:' he stuck both hands out, shaking his left wrist and shoogling the cheap-looking watch dangling on it. Wiggling the fingers on his right hand, showing off the inky marks from making all those notes over the last two days. 'I'm right-handed, see?' He dropped his arms and leaned back against the nearest pillar. Staring out into the rain. 'Far as I can make out, they've been planning it for a while. Don't know if it was the Russian mobster who *actually* killed him, or one of the Tory tosspots ... or maybe they just paid Nairn to do it? You heard Lord Fitzroy-Galbraith: "don't get to be an MP without knifing people in the back, burying the bodies, then pinning the blame on someone else". And *he's* made it all the way to the House of Lords.' A shrug. 'Whoever did it, the rest of them have closed ranks faster than you can say "dismantling the welfare state".'

Susan handed the bottle back. 'So they're going to get away with it?'

'Oh aye.' Roberta took another swig of smoky fire. 'Welcome to the wonderful world of law enforcement.' She frowned at the bottle. Bit the inside of her lip. Then held the Glenfeòrag out to Sergeant Moore. Sighed. 'Go on, then.'

He hesitated for a moment, then accepted the peace offering. Still wiped the neck before taking a hefty scoof, though. Cheeky sod. Like *he* was going to get cooties from *them*.

Soon as he swallowed, Sergeant Moore launched into a bout of coughing, wheezing, and spluttering. 'God, they give the visitors proper rotgut, don't they? Wouldn't clean my brushes with that.' He dug into his back pocket and came out with a pewter hipflask. 'Try a nip of the decent stuff.'

Roberta did. Making a point of wiping *his* cooties off first.

It went down like liquid angels.

He gestured for her to share it with Susan. 'Don't tell Customs and Excise, but a friend of a friend makes it in an undisclosed location. Might be able to set you up with a bottle or three...?' When Susan had taken a drink he hid the flask away again. 'Did you really think I'd done it?'

Roberta waggled a hand from side to side. 'Jury's still out.' She leaned back against the wall, squinting at him. 'All that crap when we went to wake up Lady Barely-Distraught, yesterday morning, and you were kidding on you thought she was dead. Meanwhile: you'd been snoring it up all night, *in her bed*, with your floppy willy?'

'Ah... Yeah.' A nod. 'Suppose I can't blame you.' Deep breath. 'But what was I supposed to do: fess up and get kicked off the case? Sir Reginald Bradbury-Scott might've been a nasty, thieving, lascivious, two-faced, condescending, stuck-up, manipulative, right-wing *wanker*, but I don't like murderers running round my patch. Never mind a whole sodding hotel full of them.' He returned their pilfered Glenfeòrag. 'Anyway, suppose I'd better go make sure PC McKinnon doesn't compromise himself *too* much. Silly sod. He means well, just a bit too eager to please.'

Sergeant Moore stepped up to the main doors. Paused. Then placed a hand on Roberta's shoulder and squeezed. 'We were never going to win, not against this lot. But at least we did our best.'

He disappeared inside and the door clunked shut. Leaving them alone with the rain.

Susan snuggled in closer, Moore's illegal moonshine warm and sweet on her breath. 'Well, *I* thought you were magnificent in there.' She wrapped an arm around Roberta's shoulders. 'Like a young Margaret Rutherford!'

The wedding bunting had faded a bit in the downpour, hanging limp and dangly like a spurned boyfriend.

That crow had another go, flapping away along the misty treetops in a swearing of disgruntled caws.

And still the rain fell.

Susan leaned in and nuzzled her ear. 'In fact, all your detecting has got me quite a-fluttered. Don't suppose you fancy...?'

Saucy minx.

Roberta let a smile crack through her frown and stood. Helped Susan up. Gave her a warm whisky kiss. And wheeched open both sides of the hotel's double doors for her. Making a big swanky gesture of it. 'We're barricading the room, though. I wouldn't trust *any* of the buggers staying here – they might have a bash tidying up their loose ends.' Hang on a minute… She paused on the threshold. 'Or do you think they'll try to bribe *me* too?'

'Would you take it if they did?'

Good question.

'Probably no'.'

A determined nod, then Susan gazed deep into her eyes. 'Then maybe *I* shouldn't either? Tell Mortimer to shove his corporate law firm up his fundamental orifice and I can be a stay-at-home mum instead?'

'Are you insane? On *my* salary?' Roberta stared at her like she'd just turned down a threesome with Keira Knightley. 'Have you seen how much Jasmine's school fees are? Never mind saving up for Naomi's. Then there's university, and we'll probably have to buy the pair of them flats as well. You stay where you are and take all the bribes you can!'

A naughty wink. 'I love it when you're masterful.'

'Have my moments. And, if you play your cards right, you'll get a few more of them in a minute. I might even struggle my way into those fancy-pants bra and knickers you like so much.'

A laugh made all the best bits of Susan jiggle. 'Be still my beating heart.' Then she smiled, one hand up to stroke Roberta's cheek. 'I do love you, you know.'

'Aye, well, don't blame you: I'm pretty damned adorable.' She slapped Susan's bum. 'Now get your pert and sexy arse up those stairs, woman!'

Because sometimes, when life screwed you over, you just had to kick it in the nadgers and go have kinky-naked-fun-time with the person you loved.

And with any luck, that person had remembered to pack the Nutella and a photograph of Keira Knightley.

Without Whom

Writing books is a strange way to make a living – involving as it does sitting on my bum, on my own, making up lies about people who don't exist. But along the way I do get to talk to and work with some lovely people, so I'd like to take this opportunity to say a massive thank you to them for helping me make this book as good as I was able.

First of all, I must thank the lovely Sarah Hodgson for working with me on the initial edit of this story before she left HarperCollins to go be a bigshot at Corvus. And to my *new* lovely editor, Fran Pathak for agreeing to publish it after all these years, assisted in this enterprise by Emily Sumner. Then there's the eagle-eyed Anne O'Brien (copy-editing) and Linda Joyce (proofreading), who helped me fix my numerous writing mistakes (any that remain are entirely my fault), and to Melissa Bond for organising them. Holly Sheldrake for shepherding the book through production; James Annal designed the cover and did all the art direction; Laura Sherlock shook the publicity tree; while Jamie Forrest, Katie Roden, and Claire Bush did the funky marketing, as did the digital team – Andy Joannou and Alex Hamnet. On the sales front: Christine Jones, Stuart Dwyer, Ellie Kyrke-Smith, Richard Green, Gillian Mackay, Charlotte Cross, and Julia Finegan rocked the UK; Leanne Williams sorted out those naughty international markets; and Gordon Kemp and Becca Souster spanked the digital realm till it couldn't remember its safety word. Becky Lloyd dealt with everything Audio. And all of these talented people at Pan Macmillan did their thing under the watchful gaze of Lucy Hale and Joanna Prior. If I've missed anyone off this list, please know that it wasn't on purpose and I think you're smashing.

I also want to thank Phil Patterson and the team at Marjacq Scripts, for helping keep my cats fed; and Allan Buchan (nee Guthrie) for being an excellent pre-reader.

Like all writers I take my hat off to the excellent librarians and booksellers, all over the world, who do so much to get books in the hands of people who need them. And let's face it, *everyone* needs books. The world would be a much better place if it contained far more readers and far fewer dickheads. Which is why YOU, the person reading this book, are a magnificent sexy beast of a thing! On behalf of every writer out there, let me say a massive THANK YOU, because without you we wouldn't be here.

I'm going to round off this gushing luvvie-fest by thanking my wife, Fiona (who has to put up with some *seriously* weird discussions while I wrestle a book together), and cats – Onion, Beetroot, and Gherkin – who don't so much help as create hairy chaos.

And last, but not least, Grendel. She was my constant companion while writing this book, way back in the LongAgo, and I couldn't have done it without her. Much loved and sorely missed.

So now, nothing remains but for me to say 'Fuck Fascism!' and I'll see you next time.